MURDER AT THE CAR RALLY: 1920S HISTORICAL COZY MYSTERY

An Evie Parker Mystery Book 3

SONIA PARIN

ISBN-10: 1091217173

ISBN-13: 978-1091217171

About this book

Lighthearted 1920s cozy mystery

She can run, but she can't hide.

When Evie Parker, Countess of Woodridge, decides to spend a day in London unaccompanied she has no idea she will encounter the one person she has hoped to spend the rest of her life avoiding. There's no escaping Isabel Fitzpatrick's exuberant energy and desire to show off her new husband. However, the encounter sets off a series of events and brings trouble right to Evie's doorstep.

Even when Evie manages to return to her country house in Berkshire, she finds the only way to avoid her childhood friend is to flee by joining a car rally group, but trouble pursues her and now a man has died under suspicious circumstances. Stranded in a small village with a group of bright young things and a killer, Evie and her bodyguard, Tom Winchester, assist Scotland Yard Detective Inspector O'Neill to unmask the mastermind behind a drug trafficking ring. A difficult task when everyone seems to be hiding something.

If you wish to receive news about my next release,
please follow me on BookBub

Chapter One

THE BEST MIRROR IS AN OLD FRIEND - GEORGE
HERBERT

Late May, 1920
Paddington Station, London

"*E*vie Parker?"

Evie performed a pirouette, swinging away from the familiar voice and using the pretext of searching her handbag to keep her gaze lowered as she strode off toward the nearest exit.

Two steps away from disappearing into the throng of fellow train passengers, a hand wrapped around her arm and pulled her back with unceremonious determination.

"Evie, it is you! Good heavens, to think I had to make a transatlantic crossing and travel to England to see you again. Isn't this marvelous? Seeing you… after all these years."

"Isabel," Evie croaked. Ten years before, when she'd left New York as a debutante, she had promised to never again utter the name of Isabel Fitzpatrick. She had almost succeeded by only saying part of her name.

"Of course, it's not really Evie Parker anymore," Isabel continued in the exuberant tone she had always employed to draw attention to herself. "Isn't it Evie Halton now? I heard you married and perished with the Titanic during your honeymoon. I'm so happy to see you didn't die."

Perished…?

Evie had been nowhere near the Titanic when it had sunk all those years ago.

Had people been saying that about her? She had just spent two years living in New York and no one had made reference to her rumored demise.

In the next instant, Isabel Fitzpatrick pinched her arm.

"Ouch!"

Isabel tilted her head back and laughed. "I had to make sure it really was you, alive and well. Think what a blast we'll have when I tell everyone how I met you at Victoria Station and pinched you to make sure you weren't a ghost."

"It's Paddington Station."

"Oh, so it is."

"What brings you to England, Isabel?" Evie forced herself to ask as she gave her arm a discreet rub.

Isabel stretched her arms out and exclaimed, "Fame and fortune, of course. I married a famous gentleman. He's a racing car driver. Don't you think that's thrilling? I do." Isabel gave her short blonde bob a flick. "Oh, the fun we have. The parties we attend. Everywhere we go, everyone knows him and photographers are always on the prowl, doing everything they can to take a photograph of us."

Evie made a point of looking around. A porter stood behind Isabel ready to transport all her luggage. But she didn't see anyone she could identify as Isabel's famous husband, Lorenzo.

While reluctant to encourage the conversation, Evie asked, "Is he traveling with you?"

"Of course. We were staying at a grand old house in the south but he had to come to London for business and now I'm joining him. Oh, we are such busy bees. Soon we'll be setting off again. We must get together. In fact, we must have lunch. I won't take no for an answer."

Evie scratched around her mind, trying to find a polite way to turn down the invitation. However, knowing Isabel would counter any attempt to say no with her own brand of persuasion, Evie abandoned her attempt and, instead, asked, "Where in the south were you staying?"

"Surrey."

Too close for comfort, Evie thought.

Isabel gestured to the porter. "I have a car waiting. It will take us straight to the Automobile Club." She gave Evie a brisk smile. "It's members only but you can come as my guest."

She then proceeded to sweep Evie out of the train station and straight into her motor car. Evie would never be able to explain how it had happened.

"Andiamo, Marco." Isabel leaned toward Evie and whispered, "My chauffeur is Italian. He doesn't speak a word of English. I just told him we should go. Isn't the Italian language beautiful? Oh, you should hear the wonderfully romantic things Lorenzo whispers in my ear. That's my husband. Lorenzo Bianchi. It all sounds like music. You know, Italians have Latin blood. Everything they do, they do with tremendous passion."

As the motor car pulled away and Isabel continued to trip over her words, Evie gazed out the window and wondered how she had ended up in Isabel's company.

She could think of someone else who would wonder...

Tom Winchester.

If Tom got wind of this he would have her head on a platter. Since her grandmother had hired him to keep an eye on her, Evie had barely left his sight. Even if she explained she knew Isabel from way back, he would perceive her as a threat; guilty until proven innocent.

Until recently, he had been parading around as her chauffeur and on two separate occasions, he had adopted the persona of Mr. Tom Winchester, independently wealthy man about town.

In reality, her grandmother had hired him as Evie's bodyguard. Evie should have objected, but if her grandmother required peace of mind, then so be it. Evie never thought of herself as being tremendously wealthy, less so since making England her home. The local gentry despised talking about money, although, they seemed to do a great deal of it behind closed doors. More so now that many estates were languishing due to poor management and lack of funds.

In any case, if her wealth posed a threat to her safety she had never noticed. Especially not now that she had Tom Winchester around to keep a close eye on her.

Since Evie had settled at her country estate, Halton

House, in Berkshire, he had remained Mr. Tom Winchester and she had lost her chauffeur.

Now that she thought about it, she could cast all blame on Tom. If he hadn't been so determined to have his way and shadow her every step, she would not have tried to elude him and she would therefore not have traveled to London by herself or bumped into Isabel.

It hadn't been that difficult to escape him. If she really thought about it, she hadn't been able to contact him...

So, yes. She felt perfectly within her rights to cast all blame at his door.

"So where are you calling home these days?" Isabel asked. "The Ritz?"

Evie scattered the storm brewing in her mind. Isabel's family had a grand house on 5th Avenue as well as a cottage in Rhode Island. Evie smiled as she recalled the first time she had described the so-called cottages to Henrietta. The dowager had been stupefied to learn some of the houses could rival any grand estate in England. Of course, Isabel would expect Evie to live in the lap of luxury.

"I'm actually not far from here." Evie waved her hand in the general direction of her town house in Mayfair. Although, after her escapade, she would be returning to her country house, but Isabel didn't need to know that.

"And what does your husband do?"

Did she honestly not know Evie had married the Earl of Woodridge? "I'm not sure." For all she knew, he spent his eternal afterlife sitting on a cloud looking down at her. Although, in life, he had been extremely industrious. Evie could well imagine him finding a métier of sorts, perhaps organizing the celestial library.

"Oh, I've heard of those marriages," Isabel commiserated in a hushed tone. "You poor thing. To think you came all the way here to only end up alone." Isabel leaned forward. "Here we are. Isn't it a splendid building? I swear the doorman is a Russian aristocrat stripped of everything after the revolution. I hear some of them have been reduced to working in service. I find that dreadfully demeaning. I'm inclined to feel sad on their behalf."

As she waited for the chauffeur to open the door, Evie plotted out an escape plan. She could excuse herself and say she needed to powder her nose and, along the way, she could bribe the maître d' to pretend she had a telephone call. Perhaps an emergency...

Shaking her head, Evie decided against the plan since no one would know where to find her. Then again... Isabel had always been so wrapped up in her life and her incessant chatter, she might miss the detail.

"We're right on time. The place fills up rather quickly but I dare say, they will always find a table for me. We made quite a splash when we arrived. A couple of photographers somehow made their way inside. Well, I suppose they greased someone's palm. I'm sure there are plenty of people willing to do just about anything for money."

Leaving the bell boy to take care of her luggage, Isabel led them toward the restaurant, all the while talking non-stop. Since she had never favored subtlety, she earned more than her share of attention.

"Oh, there he is." Isabel waved and rushed forward calling out, "Ciao, Lorenzo."

A distinguished looking man stood up and spread his arms out.

If Evie hadn't witnessed the public display of affection, she would not have believed it.

Finding the whole situation entertaining yet somewhat embarrassing, Evie looked away. She wished she hadn't because before she knew what was happening, a pair of strong arms wrapped around her with a torrent of Italian thrown in for good measure.

If that weren't enough, several flashes exploded around her.

"I told you," Isabel chirped. "Isn't it marvelous?"

～

The next day…
Halton Station, Berkshire

Evie nudged the cuff of her sleeve and checked the time. Before leaving London, she had telephoned ahead and had given her maid, Caro, strict instructions to send Edmonds to fetch her.

Knowing Caro disapproved of Tom's transformation into Mr. Tom Winchester, Evie knew she could trust Caro to keep her request a secret.

"What could be taking Edmonds so long?" she murmured under her breath. The stable hand had been champing at the bit for a chance to prove himself. Didn't he realize she'd given him the perfect opportunity to impress her? He had done a splendid job driving her to the station but he now had to prove he could be consistent.

She heard the roar of a motor car approaching and looked up only to cringe.

Tom's red roadster came to an abrupt stop. He sat staring at her, his hands gripping the steering wheel, his mouth set into a grim line.

At times, Evie thought he seemed to forget he worked for her. Although, strictly speaking, his arrangement was with her grandmother. In any case, there were quite a few people in her employ who enjoyed taking liberties and expressing their displeasure or opinions willy-nilly.

She had a good mind to put an end to it all...

Watching his approach, she tried to gauge his mood. Dressed in his country squire suit in a light shade of gray, his hair looked slightly windswept. As for his eyes... they were narrowed into slits suggesting he meant business.

Evie savored the moment. She wanted nothing more than to put his nose out of joint...

Chewing her own bone of contention, Evie imagined he had intercepted Edmonds and had raced out to fetch her from the train station.

When he reached her, Evie employed her breeziest tone to say, "Mr. Tom Winchester, fancy meeting you here."

He uttered a grumble and, slipping his hands in his pockets, he said, "Imagine my surprise when I called on you this morning and your butler told me you had decided to spend a day in town."

"Edgar said that? I shall have to have a word with him. I simply cannot have my butler distributing information about my whereabouts to just anyone." Had that been Edgar's way of expressing his dissatisfaction? She had dragged him away from the London house to step in while Mr. Crawford attended to his sick sister. While Edgar had not complained, as the days wore on without any changes to the arrangement, she had noticed Edgar becoming more restrained than usual, clearly reserving his opinions on the matter.

Until now.

What if Edgar used his role as butler to make Evie's life difficult until she released him of his duties and allowed him to return to London? Heavens, what would he do when he learned Mr. Crawford would not be returning to Halton House? Evie hadn't received confirmation, but she strongly suspected her country house butler wished to retire…

Tom looked one way and then the other. Finally, he locked his eyes with Evie's. "What on earth were you thinking, going off on your own? You didn't even take Caro with you."

"Needs must. I tried to reach you but you were nowhere to be found…" That had prompted Evie to prove to Tom she didn't need a bodyguard shadowing her every step. Certainly not if she had to go chasing after him.

She could tell her blithe remark had him grinding his back teeth and yet, the edge of his lip appeared to want to break into a smile.

"I take it you're cross with me," he said.

Evie tapped her foot. "I find myself partial to the sentiment. You see, I have lost my chauffeur and gained a certain Mr. Winchester. Would you mind telling me what your current occupation is?"

His jaw muscles twitched. "Nothing has changed." Sighing, he added, "Is that why you went off in a huff?"

Evie huffed. "I do not huff."

"You do, on occasion."

"Fine, but only when I am given reason to huff."

He looked down but she could still see his smile.

"I'm sorry to be the source of your discontentment." He gestured toward the roadster. "May I drive you home?"

Lifting her chin, Evie gave an insouciant shrug. "Yes, I suppose you may. I have no idea what could have happened to Edmonds. Am I supposed to adjust to new circumstances and carry on without a chauffeur or should I consider learning to drive myself?"

Tom held the passenger door open for Evie who took her time settling into her seat.

"At the risk of repeating myself, we never did get around to discussing our new arrangement," she continued.

Tom settled into the driver's seat. "You know as well as I do I can't go back to being your chauffeur now. What would Henrietta and Sara say?"

The dowagers would require a great deal of explaining and then dismiss the strange arrangement as an American oddity.

Tom brushed his hand across his chin. "Come to think of it, I see no reason why we couldn't let them in on the secret."

"I do."

He turned to look at her. "Name one good reason why we can't be honest with them."

"It would complicate matters and… and confuse them." It had already confused her maid and Caro had shown no qualms about expressing her displeasure.

Like all great houses in England, Halton House

employed many people who took great pride in ensuring everything ran smoothly. Everyone had a role to play. Her maid's frustration stemmed from the fact everyone knew their place. In her opinion, lines of distinction existed for a reason. Blurring those lines could disrupt the well-oiled machine and inspire chaos in an otherwise orderly world.

"Are you honestly going to say they wouldn't get past the idea of me being on a different social scale?"

Eventually, they might, but it would take a lot of explaining. In reality…

She rather liked having Mr. Winchester around and the dowagers had already accepted him as her child-hood friend.

Evie slanted her gaze toward him and wondered about his so-called social scale.

He had been able to procure items with such ease, Evie had come to believe his story about striking it lucky in the Oklahoma oilfields as something more real than the fictitious cover story it had been intended to be.

"I think we should abandon the idea of you resuming your duties as my chauffeur." She gave a firm nod. "There. I've made the decision."

"And how will I explain my constant presence?"

He had a point. The dowagers, Sara and Henrietta, had chosen to move out of the manor and into the dower house. So, he couldn't stay at Halton House, certainly not while she lived there alone.

Staring straight ahead, she said, "Home, please." After her hectic overnight stay in London, she found herself looking forward to some peace and quiet.

Tom changed the subject by asking, "Did you enjoy your day in London?"

She wanted to tell him all about her horrendous experience but feared she would get an earful of disapproval for allowing someone to kidnap her.

Deciding to skate around the subject, she said, "I... I met an old friend." Evie used the term loosely. In their youth, she and Isabel had run in the same social circles so there had been no avoiding Isabel's little jabs. It seemed some people could not restrain their need to be competitive. And Evie couldn't think of anyone more competitive than a debutante. Now that Isabel had married... Well, she appeared to be determined to prove she had done better than anyone else. "Isabel Fitzpatrick. We had lunch."

"And?" he prompted.

"And... we talked." Or, rather, she had listened to the most tedious conversation she'd ever heard about motor vehicles. "Did you know there is a gentleman who goes by the name of Count Zborowski. He's a racing driver and automobile engineer and has designed a motor car and named it the Chitty-Bang-Bang. He claims it will be the fastest and most successful vehicle to ever race at Brooklands."

"That's a strange conversation to have with your friend. Is she a motor enthusiast?"

"To tell you the truth, I'm not sure. Her husband races so I suppose she's trying to take an interest and be supportive."

Evie looked out across the fields and saw sheep dotting the landscape and a rider galloping in the distance. All the while, she tried to remember if she'd ever expressed excitement for any of Nicholas' projects. He'd had many and he'd often talked about them. While she'd listened, she'd never felt the urge to become involved in any way. However, her lack of participation could never be used to measure her affection for him. In fact, two years after his death, she still felt Nicholas would always be the love of her life…

"Where is Brooklands exactly?" she asked.

"Not far. About twenty miles away, in Surrey."

"How do you know that?"

Tom shrugged. "I'm sure I had a conversation about it with someone or other at the pub."

Evie rolled her eyes. The pub…

"You cannot possibly continue to live at the Woodridge Arms. I shall ask the dowagers to move back, then no one will be able to question your presence at Halton House."

"And will I become your permanent house guest?" He chortled. "I think that will invite remarks about fish smelling."

"Nonsense." Evie looked up and saw Halton House coming into view.

Her country pile sat in the middle of a large park with the woods in the distance.

"The house needs more than one person living in it." She wanted to enjoy the peace and quiet of country living, but sometimes, too much quiet could become predictable and tedious.

Shading her eyes, she leaned forward. "Am I expecting visitors?"

"You seem to be and quite a number of them, by the looks of it," Tom said and slowed down.

"What are you doing?"

He gave a small shrug. "That looks like trouble."

She had to agree. There appeared to be two…

three… make that five motor cars parked in front of the colonnaded entrance to Halton House.

Squinting her eyes, she thought she could just make out Edgar swinging from one side to the other. If she had to guess, she'd say her butler was trying to contain a situation.

Evie cleared her throat. "D-drive on."

"You don't sound overly confident."

Her eyebrows hitched up. Edgar now appeared to be flapping his arms.

Brushing his hand across the steering wheel, Tom said, "If you want my opinion, I would say that definitely looks like trouble and we should steer clear of it."

"But that's my doorstep." Sitting back, Evie waved her hand. "I think we'll have to meet trouble head-on. Drive on, please."

Chapter Two

"*C*ountess Woodridge." The young man approached Evie oozing charm and exemplary politeness. "I'm Lord Hemsworth. My friends call me Batty." He proceeded to introduce the rest of the entourage, most of whom had titles with the exception of a few, including a young woman named Unique.

Title or no title they appeared to have another characteristic in common. They all looked downright bizarre.

A young man wore a top hat with rabbit ears protruding from it. Another one sported an eyepatch but she caught him lifting it a couple of times, suggesting he used it as nothing more than a decorative piece.

Lord Hemsworth continued with the introductions, finishing with, "Lark Wainscot and Edward Spencer."

Edward Spencer inclined his head. Dressed in a sailor top with a skirt that actually looked like trousers, Lark Wainscot and another young woman who wore a top hat took a bow as if making an appearance on the stage.

Evie knew her quiet day in the country would have to be postponed.

Lord Hemsworth continued by explaining, "We were on our way to participate in a car rally and now it seems we have lost one of our members. Last we heard from her, she'd been staying with you."

Evie gasped. "Phillipa Brady? Has something happened to her?"

"No. No. She has simply ended up lost somewhere. I wonder if we might impose on your kindness and rest here a while. We have spent the last two weeks driving all over the southern counties to no avail."

"Of course, you are very welcome." Turning to her butler, Evie said, "Edgar, it seems we have guests for lunch. Could you make the necessary arrangements, please?"

Tom rounded the roadster. "Are you sure about that?" he murmured. "What do you know about them?"

"I remember Phillipa mentioning some of them." Only a few weeks before, Evie had given the young Australian traveler, Phillipa Brady, shelter when her motor car had broken down. She had been on her way to a car rally and now Evie's unexpected guests had provided the same explanation.

"I'm going to change out of these clothes. Tom, please keep them company."

"You mean, keep an eye on them."

"Yes, that too." Phillipa had told her about taking part in treasure hunts, which sometimes involved looking for objects in manor houses; something that had intrigued Evie at the time. Not so now.

She strode into the house and made her way up the stairs. Tapping her hand along the banister, she wondered if Phillipa had left something behind… something for the others to find.

Her attention flitted to every object she encountered along the way as if she were subconsciously taking stock of her possessions and also looking for anything that might appear to be out of place.

"I think the joke is on me," she murmured as she strode into her bedroom where she found her maid hard at work. "Caro! I see you have anticipated my needs."

Caro had laid out a lovely spring ensemble consisting of an oyster shell gray skirt and a pretty blouse with tiny primroses printed on it.

"Did you enjoy your stay in London, milady?"

Sighing, Evie removed her hat and said, "Not as much as I had hoped. I'm afraid my plan to annoy Mr. Winchester backfired on me."

"How so, milady?"

Evie rolled her eyes. "Some would say I got my just deserts. As I made my way out of the train station, an old friend saw me. I use the term loosely since we were never that close but we ran in the same circles. Isabel Fitzpatrick reigned supreme in most of them. She has a way about her and I have never quite figured out what it is." Suffice to say, Evie thought, it took a great deal of patience to be with her.

"Some people light up the room and that seems to be enough to draw others to them," Caro said.

"No, that's not it. For starters, she is an incessant and at times painful chatterbox. She has an opinion about everything and, let me tell you, her opinions are not always pleasant. She thought I had gone down with the Titanic."

Caro gasped. "I hope you set her straight."

It took a moment for Caro's remark to register, when it did, Evie noticed her maid smiling. "Laugh if you must. It wasn't enough for her to see me in the flesh. She actually had to prove I lived. Look, she left a mark on my arm. I should have her up for assault."

"Oh, you have a mark on your other arm too," Caro observed.

Evie gasped. "Make that assault and battery. This is where she grabbed me and coerced me to go with her."

"I hope you were able to escape her clutches."

"I'm afraid not. She has the force of a tornado." Pushing out a breath, Evie added, "At least I got a nice meal out of it. Although, there is no such thing as a free lunch. I had to listen to her endless prattling about being married to a famous racing car driver and how they travel everywhere." Evie sat down at her dressing table and cupped her chin in her hand. "And here I am complaining about it all. I believe I'm growing old before my time."

Caro smiled. "Did you at least manage to put Tom's nose out of joint?"

"I think I did. Although…" Why had she ever bothered?

The day before, she had woken up feeling quite annoyed at having to telephone Tom at the pub. When she had, he hadn't been there to take her call. She had felt inconvenienced… and something else. Something she couldn't quite put her finger on. "I think I should learn to drive."

Caro's eyes widened. "Really? Is that even allowed?"

"Pardon? Of course, it is. Phillipa drives. Why shouldn't I?"

"Because you have a chauffeur."

"That's just it. I don't."

"What about Edmonds? He is ever so happy about his new uniform."

"Well… I suppose there will be occasions when I'll need a chauffeur. After all, it wouldn't look right for Tom to drive the large motor car with me in the back seat."

"Why not? He did before."

Yes, but everything had changed now…

"We might play it by ear." Evie got up and removed her coat.

"I saw some of your new guests. They look… exuberant."

They certainly were. Ever since the war had ended, it seemed people wished to celebrate every moment they lived. The press had labeled them the 'bright young things' and then there were the flappers.

Whatever name the new generation of misfits chose to go by, they all had one trait in common. They all thrived on their desire to flaunt their disdain for acceptable behavior and were quite determined to make their mark in the world by blazing their way through every single day, living for the moment.

"I like a bit of excitement every now and then but I'm not sure I would fit in with a group of people who thrive on it," Evie mused. "I would certainly struggle to keep up. There's a lot to be said for quiet moments of reflection…"

Caro seemed to find the remark odd. She tilted her head from side to side and said, "You would fare a lot better than I would. I hope they know how to behave."

"I have no doubt they do." But, would they? "There are several titled ladies and gentlemen in the group and the others come from well to-do families. Although, that doesn't necessarily guarantee they will behave. In any case, they'll be making their way after luncheon."

Evie inspected her hair and adjusted a few wayward locks. She had meant to do something about it in London but Isabel had commandeered all her time. "Any news from the dowagers?"

Caro nodded. "I didn't see them myself, but Mrs. Arnold said they spent some time in the attic. Apparently, they'd been looking for a vase."

"Did they find it?"

"I believe they did. The housekeeper said she wrote a list of everything they took. The footmen were kept busy for several hours loading up the pieces of furniture."

Evie's eyebrows shot up. "What do you suppose they want with it all? The dowager house is beautifully furnished."

"Are you really asking me, milady?"

"No, I'm speaking out loud. I suppose I shall have to pay them a visit. Perhaps this is their way of leaving a calling card. I haven't seen them in over a week. It's not as if I have been busy… and I'm sure they haven't really been busy. Or have they?"

"I believe your curiosity has been piqued."

"Yes, you might be right. Only…" she gave Caro an impish smile, "I'm almost afraid to satisfy my curiosity."

Chapter Three

GUESTS, LIKE FISH, BEGIN TO SMELL AFTER THREE
DAYS - BENJAMIN FRANKLIN

The dower house

"I hear you had some guests for lunch today," Henrietta said.

Evie took a sip of her tea and, finding much delight in the beverage, especially as she could employ it to stall for time, she took another.

The dowager displayed tremendous patience holding Evie's gaze for several seconds before applying her eyebrow to gradually make a point.

Evie watched it rise by increments until she thought it would reach the dowager's hairline.

Finally, Evie gave a small nod. "It's a group of motor car enthusiasts making their way to Portsmouth. They're quite a jovial lot."

"And where do you know them from?"

Evie looked down at her cup and found it to be

empty, which meant she couldn't use it as a delay tactic. "May I have some more tea, please?"

"Certainly."

Henrietta didn't move. It seemed her tea came at a price.

Setting the cup down on the dainty table between them, Evie said, "They mentioned knowing Phillipa. It seems she missed their rendezvous point and they have been searching for her ever since."

Henrietta gasped. "Phillipa Brady? Missing?"

"I had the same reaction but she knows where she is. Or rather… she sent me a note a couple of days ago to thank me for my hospitality. She's in Northampton."

"But that's in the opposite direction."

"Yes, I believe there has been some sort of miscommunication."

Henrietta chortled. "So, does anyone know where everyone is supposed to be headed?"

"It would seem so, yes. I didn't really ask. I suppose one has to assume they know where they will eventually end up." Evie looked at the teapot. She knew it would be rude to help herself, at least, in this instance.

When invited to tea at the dowager's house, Henrietta insisted on being at the helm. Her butler stood by, the edge of his lip slightly raised. Evie tried to catch his attention but he appeared to be oblivious of his surroundings.

"Lord Hemsworth is among the party," Evie said. "I believe you know his grandmama."

"Why is it everyone assumes I only know people over a certain age?"

"I beg your pardon, perhaps he meant his mother."

"Oh, no. You're quite right. I do know Lady Louise.

Her brother spent some time in America or the Caribbean. I forget which."

Glancing around the pretty drawing room, Evie did a double take. "Is that a new vase?"

Henrietta barely glanced at it. "No, not really... It's been in the family for generations. I'm surprised you noticed it." Henrietta reached for the teapot and tipped it slightly to pour some tea into Evie's cup, only to stop and say, "So... You bid your guests farewell."

That tea couldn't come soon enough.

Evie took a deep swallow. "Well..."

Henrietta tipped the teapot a fraction, enough for a trickle of tea to cascade into the cup.

"Not exactly."

Henrietta set the teapot down. "What do you mean?"

Evie stared at the teacup and wondered if one sip would be enough.

"I showed them Phillipa's letter and, after contacting her at the pub where she's staying, they decided to try another rendezvous."

Henrietta poured another few drops into the cup enticing Evie to add, "Everyone thought it would be easier if Phillipa found her way back to Halton House."

That earned her another few drops of tea.

"Someone suggested meeting her half way, but as they are all headed down south, it really made more sense to wait for her to arrive."

Seeing the cup now half full, Evie dug deep and told the dowager about Isabel Fitzpatrick.

"Can you believe she thought I had perished with the Titanic?"

That earned her a full cup of tea.

Brightened by the tidbit, Henrietta exclaimed, "Is she slow-witted?"

"Not at all."

"Then she must have been taking a stab at you, my dear. If I had to read into it, I'd say she thinks of you as inconsequential. Or, rather, she is trying to slot you into that box." Henrietta clicked her fingers. "Out of sight, out of mind. You must pose some sort of threat to her. Were you very good friends with her?"

Evie smiled. "Before I went down with the ship?"

Henrietta shivered. "I wouldn't joke about such matters. Certainly not if you're planning another trip any time soon."

"In truth, I always tried to avoid her. She has this way about her that sets me on edge. On the one hand, she appears to be complimenting you, yet when you think about what she says, you realize she's just subjected you to a thorough verbal assault."

"Well then, you must keep your distance from her," Henrietta suggested.

Evie relaxed back into her chair to enjoy her hard-earned tea.

"I see Mr. Winchester is still around."

Ah yes, Evie thought, remembering the purpose of her visit. "Henrietta, I need to ask a favor of you."

Evie had never known manipulating people could be so exhausting.

"Milady! Is something the matter?" Caro asked as she entered Evie's boudoir and found her stretched out on the chaise lounge where she had collapsed after her walk from the dower house in the village nearby.

Evie managed to sit up. She plumped up the cushions and nodded. "Yes, I'm perfectly fine. I suppose it's too early to change for dinner."

Agreeing with a small nod, Caro said, "I came up thinking I would get an early start sorting out your evening clothes. I would have thought your guests would keep you quite busy."

Busy to the point of making her feel old. Being only in her mid-thirties, she simply couldn't allow that to happen.

"When I returned from my visit to the dowager, I strode into the library and found them playing golf using umbrellas as golf clubs, while the rest were busy organizing a human pyramid."

Caro laughed. "It must be wonderfully thrilling to be able to provide your own entertainment."

"I'm not so sure about that. One of them proposed we play a murder mystery game. He's a writer and quite keen to pen his first book. Apparently, we are all to appear in it. I only hope I don't turn up dead. Once in a week is enough for me."

When Caro gasped, she told her about Isabel Fitzpatrick only to realize she had already mentioned her to Caro. "Heaven help me. She is becoming quite the topic of conversation with me and to think I had promised never to utter her name again."

"Is she really that disagreeable?"

Evie gave a weary nod. "In an underhanded sort of way. I hope I've seen the last of her. She's staying in London for a few days and then heading back to Brooklands. That is far too close for comfort."

Evie closed her eyes and tried to work out the distance between the village of Halton and Brooklands. Then she entertained a worst-case scenario and pictured herself fleeing in the opposite direction.

"By the way, Lady Sara is moving back to Halton House." And now, Evie thought, Mr. Winchester could move out of the pub and establish himself at Halton House.

"Not Lady Henrietta?" Caro asked.

"No and I get the feeling she planned this all along. Don't ask why but she seemed overly excited by the prospect of having the dower house all to herself. It never occurred to me to wonder how the two dowagers were getting on in the one house. They have both been mistress of Halton House at different times. I imagine they now share the responsibilities at the dower house." One house, two mistresses. Evie shook her head. She would have to tread with care and make some inquiries…

"If there had been friction, I'm sure one or the other would have mentioned it," Caro suggested.

"True." Although, half the time, they expected Evie to work their cryptic messages out for herself. Leaning back, she threw her arm over her face. "I think this is the most excitement I can take."

Hearing a knock at the door, Evie sat up.

Edgar strode in, handed Caro an envelope, and then left.

"There's a telegram for you, milady."

"Did Edgar just leave? He usually likes to handle everything properly and wait for a response."

"I believe he is somewhat flustered by your guests,

milady. He doesn't appear to know if he's coming or going."

"How odd. He's usually so well composed." She hoped his odd behavior didn't have anything to do with Mr. Crawford's prolonged absence.

Reading the telegram, Evie surged to her feet. "Caro. Pack my bags, please."

Chapter Four

THE COWARD'S WAY OUT

"What do you mean we're leaving?" Tom asked.

Evie accepted a drink from Edgar. Her eyebrows lifted slightly. "Edgar? What is this?"

"A Bee's Knees, my lady." He glanced over his shoulder and murmured, "One of your guests commandeered the drinks' cabinet and took it upon himself to prepare some cocktails."

"I see, and what is in a Bee's Knees?"

"It contains gin, honey and lemon juice. If that is not satisfactory, I can organize something else, my lady."

"Thank you, Edgar. This will be fine." Glancing around the drawing room, she made sure everyone had a drink.

"You were about to explain why we're leaving," Tom prompted.

"Oh, yes. It seems we have no choice. We must leave. We'll drive out early tomorrow. I have already instructed Caro to pack a bag for me, although, knowing Caro, she'll organize several trunks."

"And what about your guests?"

"Sara will be here." Evie glanced over at her mother-in-law. "She looks quite comfortable chatting with everyone."

Tom accepted a glass of whisky from Edgar. He held Evie's gaze for a long moment before asking, "What brought this about? Has something happened? I want to say you are not known for your erratic decisions but you know I can't, certainly not after your recent escapade in town. Regardless, this seems rather hasty."

"I'd like to know how she found out where I live," Evie mused. "She's only just arrived in London. Why would she want to leave so soon?"

"Are you talking about someone I know?" Tom asked.

"Yes, of course. I mean… No. Must I say her name?"

"I see. You're referring to your friend, Isabel Fitzpatrick."

"You know Isabel?" someone sitting nearby asked.

Turning, Evie tried to remember the young man's name.

"Lord Braithwaite," he offered. "Charlie to my friends."

Charlie wore the most outrageous vest with too many colors to name. Evie couldn't detect a particular pattern. It looked as if someone had fired a revolver at him loaded with paint.

"Yes," Tom answered. "Lady Woodridge is referring to Isabel."

Charlie looked impressed. "You know she's married to Lorenzo Bianchi. He recently placed in the Indianapolis 500."

"He did what and where?" Evie asked.

"It's a race," Tom explained. "It's held at Speedway in Indiana."

"If Lorenzo Bianchi is here then that means he won't be racing this year," Charlie said, his tone excited. "I know some car racers who'll be happy to hear the news."

Reading Evie's blank expression, Tom said, "The race is scheduled for May 31, Decoration Day."

Charlie's eyes brimmed with enthusiasm. "I hear there's a car with an eight-cylinder engine this year. What I'd give to be there…"

Evie switched off and when the conversation continued to focus on too many numbers, cylinders, speed and such, she slipped away and left Tom to enjoy his conversation with his new bosom friend.

Accepting another drink from Edgar, she turned her thoughts to her decision.

Would a hasty retreat or, rather, an exodus be perceived as cowardly? While she didn't particularly like the idea of being run out of her own home, she couldn't see any other way to avoid Isabel Fitzpatrick. She needed to do this. For her own peace of mind and… and sanity.

Then again, she couldn't leave Sara to deal with her unexpected guests. They were her responsibility.

Her mess, her clean-up, Evie thought. Although… "A problem shared is a problem halved."

She glanced over at Sara but before she could work up the courage to ask if she wouldn't mind looking after the car rally group, Edgar gave her the signal and announced dinner.

As they all made their way to the dining room, Evie's focus remained on her dilemma. Duty demanded she face up to her responsibility. However, self-preservation nudged her in the opposite direction…

She anticipated a long night ahead with much tossing and turning.

Batty, the guest sitting next to her, said, "Lady Woodridge, we hear you were recently involved in a murder case."

"Deep in the thick of it," Evie heard Sara murmur.

"Hardly that," Evie said, "I like to think of myself as an accidental bystander."

"But you assisted the police with their investigation," Batty continued.

"On several occasions, we happened to be in the same room and exchanged views." In fact, she had been interrogated twice… "How did you ever hear about it?" The crime had been reported in the local papers, but her name had been kept out. As far as she knew, no one had officially linked her to the murders. Of course, rumors had abounded…

One of the women in the group joined in the conversation, saying, "A friend of ours collects stories about crimes. He's intrigued by everything that remains in the background."

Evie remembered Batty introducing her as Lark Wainscot.

Batty added, "What you might call, the underbelly. In his opinion, we read reports about a crime committed in a small village but no one goes into any real depth."

"What more information could you possibly want?" Sara asked.

Batty explained, "Something to make the story more vibrant and, dare I say, relatable."

Intrigued, Sara asked, "How do you expect to relate to a murder?"

"The victims were real people with lives and families," Batty explained. "Their names were not released. We assume the families wished to keep detailed information private, but that only raises questions."

"Heavens, and how does your friend get information?" Sara asked.

"He has his ways."

Evie wondered if the village of Halton had informers eager to share gossip, possibly as a way of putting the little village on the map or perhaps even for personal gain. She knew Lady Henrietta relied on her butler's popularity with the local maids to get her tidbits but she went looking for it. Did someone make it their business to broadcast behind the scene news?

"Does your friend visit places where crimes have been committed?" she asked.

Batty smiled. "That would be telling."

A good reporter never revealed his sources. Where had she heard that before?

Lark Wainscot made eye contact with Evie and gave her a brisk smile. "From what we understand, you were quite helpful, providing the police with some leads. How did you come by them?"

Hadn't she already answered that question?

"You must excel at deductive thinking," Lark continued. "Or, you must have quite a nose for criminal activities."

"Neither, I'm sure." Evie smiled. "Perhaps I am a little observant. It does go a long way."

Deciding it would be best to change the subject, Evie asked, "How often do you hold these car rallies?" Glancing around the table she noticed Tom smiling at her. Yes, she thought, she had asked for a reason. She had changed the subject but she also wished to find out if Batty could be the go-between. Traveling around the country to attend car rallies could be his cover, hiding his true identity as a roving reporter.

"As often as we can. In fact, we have been at it for nearly six months now. Once we reach our destination, we decide to set off somewhere else."

"That's quite an exciting life you lead." Never quite knowing where one might end up, she thought. Always waking up to a new view outside their window.

"And yet, we have never found ourselves in the midst of a murder investigation," Unique piped in. "We must be doing something wrong. I would give anything to be involved in a mystery."

Evie took a sip of her wine. "I wouldn't recommend going in search of a murder case. They can be gruesome and... disconcerting."

"Yes, but think of the experience," Unique insisted. "I need to feed my writer's curiosity."

"Find something else to write about," Evie suggested.

Charlie, Lord Braithwaite, shook his head. "Readers enjoy murder mysteries. I'm not sure what that says about them."

"Perhaps," Evie said, "they wish to keep crime at bay by delegating it to the realms of fiction."

"I read because I wish to be transported," Unique offered. "And I want to experience something new, something outside of my scope of experience."

"How anyone can find joy from a dreary murder is beyond me," Sara murmured.

Evie noticed she had been doing a great deal of murmuring and wondered if it had something to do with expressing her disapproval over the new breed of people. Or…

Had something happened at the dower house to put her in a mood and lower her tolerance?

Had she drawn the short straw? Evie had asked Henrietta if she would like to move back to Halton House. Instead, Sara had moved in. She hoped it hadn't been against her wishes.

"How do you pass your time, Lady Sara?" Charlie asked.

Smiling, Sara offered, "I have much to occupy myself with."

"Tea parties, genteel soirees, dinners, with some sport thrown in to fill in the gaps," Unique said. "There has to be more to life."

Sara raised her glass and defended her choices, "As I have nothing to prove, I am perfectly content to enjoy my country pursuits."

"No one is faulting you for it, Lady Sara. You lead a ritualistic lifestyle." Unique shrugged. "It serves your purpose. But if you wish to experience something new, you have to break away from everything you know and sometimes go where angels fear to tread."

Sara smiled. "Since my purpose is to live a life of peace and relative quiet, I would much rather dwell within my safe cocoon."

Fearing the conversation might turn into an argument, Evie said, "I should very much like to participate in a car rally. I think it sounds like a lot of fun, but how is it all organized? Where do you spend your evenings? Where do you sleep?"

Unique laughed. "What if it rains? You get wet."

Alexander, Lord Saunders, said, "We play it by ear."

Evie looked up from her meal. Lord Saunders had changed into a formal dinner suit. Instead of black, it had been completely fashioned in red and black tartan...

Alexander continued, "If we can't find a pub then, at any given time, one of us will usually know someone in the vicinity who might be willing to put us up for the night. One of our hosts referred to us as traveling troubadours happy to sing for our supper."

Evie rather liked the sound of that, but she didn't think she had the ability to barge in on someone unannounced.

Despite the one exception, namely Isabel, Evie thought she would enjoy having a group of people dropping in every now and then. It could certainly break up the rhythm that could sometimes feel tedious and repetitive.

Glancing up, she saw a footman enter. He strode up to Edgar and delivered a message. Edgar in turn, approached Evie, one eyebrow slightly raised.

With her attention engaged, Evie leaned back.

"Begging your pardon, my lady. There is someone at the door."

Evie's heart jumped to her throat. She snatched her wine glass and gulped down the contents.

Surely not. Surely not. It couldn't be Isabel Fitzpatrick.

"W-who is it, Edgar?" If he uttered Isabel's name, she would… she would be perfectly entitled to say she was not at home. But it couldn't be Isabel. She had only just sent a telegram saying she would be arriving early the next day.

Edgar whispered, "Miss Phillipa Brady."

At the sound of the name, Evie surged to her feet nearly sending her chair toppling back. "Would you excuse me, please." She rushed out of the dining room. Once she reached the entrance hall, she spread her arms out. "Phillipa. You have no idea how glad I am to see you." Evie threw her arms around her.

"Oh, happy to oblige." Phillipa laughed. "I've never had such a welcome before."

"We're having dinner. Come in and join us and tell us how you managed to drive down so quickly. Where have you been? I mean, I know you were staying at some pub or other and that's how the others were able to contact you… Oh, heavens. It's so good to see you. Everyone's been looking for you. Oh, I can't wait to hear all about your adventures as I'm sure you have had many." Realizing her words were tripping over each other, Evie stopped and scooped in a big breath. She hoped she hadn't caught the Isabel bug…

Turning, she saw Edgar standing by the dining room door. "Edgar, please set a place at the table for Miss Brady. Oh…" She turned to Phillipa again. "You've been traveling. I suppose you want to freshen up."

"Yes, I wouldn't mind. I'm rather dusty and weary."

"I'm just so glad to see you." Evie sighed with relief. "Edgar will show you to your room."

Evie returned to the dining room and made the

happy announcement, which everyone celebrated with raised glasses.

After that, Evie could barely eat a bite. She couldn't explain her excitement. As they moved to the drawing room for after dinner drinks and coffee, Evie asked Edgar to bring some champagne. "We must celebrate Phillipa's arrival properly."

"You'd think the Prince of Wales had descended upon us," Sara murmured as she sat beside Evie.

Smiling, Evie said, "Really, I would have expected you to be more impressed by a visit from the King himself."

"Yes, well… that's what I meant but when you reach my age, you tend to make an effort to connect to the younger generation. It doesn't always work…"

"Your age doesn't happen to be very old, mama. Fifty is a glamorous age. You've lived a little and you have much to live for."

"I think that's the first time you've called me mama without hesitating. You're as giddy as a child on Christmas morning. What's come over you?"

Her world had tilted back into balance. She wouldn't have to face Isabel again. "At the risk of coming across as being somewhat churlish, now Phillipa is here, I can go ahead with my exodus. As Henrietta would say, tally-ho."

Sara gasped. "And what exactly am I to do with your unwanted guest? What do I say to her?"

Oh… Evie hadn't thought of that.

"I am sorry, Evangeline, but I am not going to lie. Not even for you."

"You don't have to. You can tell her… I have gone on an impromptu trip and will be traveling for quite some time. It's what I'm doing and, in truth, I'm not really sure when I will return…"

"You seem to forget yourself, my dear. You are the Countess of Woodridge. Therefore, you will return in time to organize the Hunt Ball."

"Oh… Yes, of course."

Chapter Five

A JOURNEY OF A THOUSAND MILES BEGINS WITH A FLAT TIRE

*T*om took his place next to Evie at the breakfast table. Despite the late night, his eyes sparkled. "Any sign of Phillipa?"

"Yes, I sent Caro to check on her. She apologizes profusely for falling asleep last night."

In the end, they had celebrated without her. And, in the midst of it all, Evie had asked if they could join the car rally. The hasty decision had been made out of desperation and she hoped she wouldn't have to repent at leisure. Evie also hoped their late night wouldn't delay their departure.

"Did you enjoy your dinner conversations last night? You seemed to be holding a deep and meaningful discussion with the woman sitting next to you."

"Marjorie," Tom said.

"Plain Marjorie? Everyone else seems to have a pseudonym or some sort of fanciful pet name."

"Yes, plain Marjorie. She's actually a keen golfer. So, we talked at length about the game."

"You play golf?"

Tom nodded.

Evie set her fork down. Why hadn't she known? And…

Why did Marjorie have something in common with Tom?

"It must have been refreshing for you to chat with someone about a subject you are passionate about." To think, when he'd first started pretending to be her chauffeur, he'd barely said a word to her, even when Evie had tried her very best to engage him in conversation.

"I enjoyed it."

And? Evie held his gaze as a way of prompting him for more information.

"She's thinking of writing a murder mystery set in a golfing tournament."

Another writer.

"I am beginning to wonder if I have been condemned to live among people intent on killing. Where is this obsession with murder coming from?"

Tom took his time chewing his bacon. "You've found it somewhat entertaining. Didn't you refer to recent events as solving a puzzle?"

"I don't recall saying that to you."

He shrugged. "I'm sure it came up in conversation."

Her guests began to trickle into the breakfast room, most heading straight for the coffee.

Evie watched the parade and wondered if they were trying to make a statement with their haphazard style of dressing.

Unique had chosen a striped blouse with a polka dot skirt in contrasting colors of orange and blue. One of the gentlemen wore a cricketing outfit mismatched with a dinner jacket. Another one had applied a great deal of pomade to his hair and had styled it into waves curving across his forehead. Lark Wainscot and one other young woman had favored beige. Evie thought they were well suited for a trip to the pyramids or a safari adventure in the heart of the African continent or even a day out boating.

"Lady Woodridge. Are you still eager to join us?" Charlie asked.

Evie noticed several people looking up as if eager to hear her response.

"I most certainly am. In fact, I'm quite looking forward to the adventure. How soon do you think you'll all be ready to leave?"

Sara had chosen to breakfast with them that morning; an unusual move on the dowager's part as she normally preferred to enjoy a leisurely breakfast in bed.

She set her teacup down and said, "Evangeline, dear. If you are so eager to set off, why not get a head start and let these bright young things see if they can catch up to you?"

"I say, that would be splendid," Charlie said. "I love a challenge." Turning to Tom, he asked, "What do you drive? Oh, wait... An AC Six, the red roadster you drove in yesterday. That should give you a proper start. Will you be sharing the driving?"

Sara nearly choked on her tea. When she recovered, she mouthed, "I forbid it."

"I had no idea Lady Sara felt so strongly about female drivers," Tom murmured.

"Nor did I." Did it have something to do with a sense of decorum or did Sara worry about safety?

Batty entered the breakfast room and Charlie filled him in on their plans, going on to suggest, "We could all meet up at the Pecking Goose. Do you know it? We always stop for a rest there."

"I think Sara has set something into motion," Tom whispered, "and we're going to have to do the heavy lifting and put a decent distance between us and them."

"Admit it, you're looking forward to this." Evie helped herself to another cup of coffee thinking she would have a long wait until her next one. "Edgar, please ask Mrs. Horace to prepare some sandwiches for our journey." Leaning toward Tom, she whispered, "I have a feeling these young bucks think they can catch up to us in no time. We should give them a run for their money. Be ready to leave in a hour…"

Three hours later… On the road to nowhere.

Evie grabbed hold of Tom's arm. "Why are we limping?"

"Flat tire." Tom eased the motor car onto the side of the road and, keeping his tone casual, said, "It's as good a time as any to stop for a break."

Evie commended Tom for his bright attitude and expert handling of the vehicle only to then say, "Do you even know how to change a flat tire?"

Giving her a lifted eyebrow look, Tom held the passenger door open for Evie.

"I guess that's a yes and…" she couldn't help teasing him, "I suppose this means you wish me to stand by the side of the road."

"It might help."

She watched him take off his coat and roll up his sleeves. "Do you think I'm a coward for fleeing?"

He chortled but refrained from commenting.

"I know it seems petty, but the thought of spending another second in Isabel's company makes my head throb."

"There's your answer. You find her disagreeable and you're taking the most sensible step by putting distance between you. She's bound to get the message."

"That's just it. I'm afraid she's rather persistent." Evie crossed her arms and mused, "Know thyself. We both attended the same academy and took a class in philosophy but she must have missed that particular lesson. Isabel doesn't know the meaning of introspection and, therefore, she has no ability to scrutinize her actions."

Evie struck up a pensive pose and wondered if she thought she knew herself.

She knew enough and... she considered herself a work in progress.

The years had transformed her. Her husband had been in the prime of his life. Losing someone she'd expected to spend an entire life with had made her appreciate every moment she could experience living in joy. She simply refused to spend any of her valuable time in the presence of someone whose main aim in life seemed to be focused on making others miserable.

Evie gave a firm nod of her head.

Tom laughed. "Did you just reach a conclusion?"

"I did and I intend sticking to it." Looking into the distance, she said, "I really don't see how the others hope to catch up to us before noon. How far do you think we've traveled?" Shielding her eyes, she looked one way and then the other. "There's a sign up ahead. I think it says Waltham or maybe Popham. It's too far to see clearly."

"We've probably managed to do about sixteen miles."

Still too close for comfort, Evie thought. "Do you think they'll catch up?"

Tom laughed. "I think you're showing a competitive streak."

"Well?"

Tom brushed a hand across his brow. "They didn't look that eager to hit the road. I wouldn't be surprised if they are only now staggering toward their vehicles and making a move to leave."

Digging inside her pocket, she retrieved a list Sara had compiled for her with the names of all her friends and acquaintances who lived between the village of Halton and Portsmouth. It had been quite considerate. She imagined Sara telephoning everyone to warn them of a marauding gang of bright young things accompanied by her daughter-in-law heading their way.

Putting the list away, she turned to admire the wild-flowers growing by the side of the road but her mind couldn't settle on the simple task. "What if it happens again? You won't have a spare tire."

Tom straightened and wiped his hands clean. "You might have to embrace the spirit of adventure and not worry about such details. We'll be fine."

"You sound confident."

"That's because I am. Someone tampered with our tire and, as we are alone on the road, there is no chance of it happening again."

"What? H-how do you know someone tampered with it?"

"There's a puncture. Someone pierced it enough for it to eventually give way."

"In jest, I hope." Who could have thought of doing such a thing? "Although, I don't really see the humor in it, but I would prefer to think someone wanted to slow us down rather than... I can't even bring myself to say it." Nor could she stop herself from entertaining the thought. Did someone have malicious intentions?

"Are you sorry you came now?"

She wanted to say yes but she would not have been able to push the admission out even if she tried. This had to be a bad joke.

Her gaze fixed on the road behind them. She could see a motor car approaching and someone waving.

As the car drew nearer, Evie realized they were not waving hello. Another thought struck.

Evie recognized the person waving frantically.

Finally, she said, "Impossible."

Tom finished putting his tools away and said, "If you think about it, nothing is really impossible."

"Yes, I realize that now."

Noticing Evie's intense frown, Tom followed her gaze. "I guess someone has caught up to us."

"It's Isabel Fitzpatrick."

"Are you sure?"

"Yes. I'd recognize those blonde curls anywhere. Would you mind explaining that to me? How is it possible? She sent a telegram saying she would arrive at Halton House this morning and now she's here, on the road, heading right for us."

"Evie?"

"I'm perfectly fine if that's what you intended asking. In shock, but otherwise quite prepared... More or less."

Never mind that she had gone out of the way to avoid the woman only to have her hunt her down.

Evie pressed both hands against her cheeks. "Heavens, if I didn't know better I'd say Isabel took exception to my exodus and is intent on running us over." A few seconds later, she changed her mind. "Oh… Oh, my goodness. There's something wrong."

Tom agreed. He grabbed hold of Evie's arm and guided her away from the roadster.

"Why is the car swerving?"

They both stopped in the middle of the road. One moment the oncoming motor car appeared to be headed in one direction and in the next instant, it swerved away…

They both squinted their eyes.

"I think there's something wrong with Lorenzo and Isabel is struggling to control the steering wheel."

The vehicle didn't seem to be slowing down and yet everything appeared to be happening in slow motion.

Tom cupped his hands around his mouth and yelled out to swerve to the left. Then, at the last moment, Tom grabbed Evie by the waist and plunged them both toward the opposite side of the road.

Evie heard Isabel's scream as the vehicle careened out of control and hit the ditch with a thud followed by the sound of metal crunching up.

"Stay here." Tom scrambled to his feet and rushed toward the vehicle. Despite his warning to stay put, Evie followed and reached him in time to help pull Lorenzo and Isabel out before the car burst into flames.

Chapter Six

*E*vie did not take her eyes off the road. Not even to look at her watch. Tom would be gone for as long as it took and she knew he would be doing his best to return as quickly as he could.

Since being pulled out of the wrecked vehicle, Isabel had said next to nothing. Even when Tom had covered Lorenzo with his coat, she had only managed a light whimper.

Any minute now, Evie expected her to snap out of it and go into a state of hysterics.

Evie kept her arm around her shoulder tucking Isabel's limp body against her.

She tried to figure out how much time had elapsed. No point in checking her watch, she thought, because she didn't know what time Tom had left…

Taking a deep swallow, she risked taking her eyes off the road to look around her and then up at the sky. When they'd stopped, the sun had nearly been above them.

She glanced at the smoldering pile on the other side of the road.

Isabel didn't have a scratch on her but Evie had remembered some soldiers she had visited at the local hospital appearing to be perfectly fine while slowly succumbing to injuries suffered internally.

She looked around her and tried to take her mind off the images still lingering in her mind, to no avail.

Tom had shaken his head. Stepping away from the lifeless body, he had spent a few moments in silent intro-spection. Then he'd told Evie he needed to go for help because the alternative would be to wait for someone to drive along.

After spending some time making sure Evie would be fine coping with the situation, he'd driven off…

"An hour," Evie whispered. In reality, she reasoned it had to be less. Waiting for someone or for something to happen… focusing on it, could make time drag on. Five minutes could turn into an hour. Ten minutes into two hours.

Hearing the sound of a vehicle approaching, she sat up and looked along the road Tom had taken but she didn't see anything. So, she looked the other way. That's when she saw a white vehicle approaching.

Evie swallowed only to realize her throat felt parched.

A few minutes later, the vehicle slowed and came to a stop. Two men emerged. "Lady Woodridge?"

Evie nodded.

"We received a telephone call from the next village. Their ambulance service is in use so we were called in."

One man hurried toward Lorenzo and crouched down. After a moment, he shook his head and strode back to the ambulance. While the other man checked on Isabel.

"She's most likely in shock," he said. "We'll take her up to the hospital."

Evie made a few head gestures that even she found confusing. When the man helped Isabel to her feet, Evie rubbed the numbness away from her arm.

Feeling at a loss, she looked down the road and thought she caught sight of another vehicle approaching. It stopped behind the ambulance and a man climbed out. Tall and distinguished looking with gray hair and a smart suit.

"May I be of assistance? I'm Sir Richard Warwick." He extended his hand to help Evie to her feet.

"I'm…" Hearing another car approaching, she looked down the road and saw Tom's red roadster.

Bringing the car to a stop, he jumped out and rushed toward her. "Sorry to have taken so long."

After Tom introduced himself, Sir Warwick turned back to Evie who must have looked confused enough for Tom to make the introduction.

"This is Lady Woodridge. We'd stopped to fix a flat tire when this other motor car ran off the road."

"Lady Woodridge. Very pleased to meet you. I believe I know your mother-in-law. How is Lady Sara?"

Not surprised by the revelation as she often encountered people who knew either Sara or Henrietta, Evie forced herself to smile. "She's quite well."

"Are you all right to travel now?" Sir Warwick asked.

"We should be fine. Thank you."

The ambulance took off in the direction Tom had come from. Taking a deep swallow, Evie managed to ask, "Do they have a hospital?"

"Don't worry about that. How are you holding up?" Tom asked.

"I'm actually a bit shaken and thirsty."

Tom rushed to their roadster and retrieved a bottle of cider Mrs. Horace had packed for their lunch.

Even though she knew no one would be able to provide exact answers, she couldn't help asking, "How could this have happened?"

"Maybe the driver lost control of the vehicle," Sir Warwick suggested. "It's been known to happen. This is a well-traveled road and we've had our fair share of incidents. I daresay, the police will want to look into it."

"Yes, they've asked us to remain here until they arrive," Tom explained.

"When did you speak with the police?" Evie asked.

Tom explained, "The first person I spotted in the village turned out to be a constable."

"You were gone for quite some time."

"I had to get some gas. The pharmacy had a 'back in five minutes' sign but I had to wait half an hour for someone to open up again."

Evie took a sip of the cider and wished she could have something stronger to drink.

"Did Isabel say anything at all?" Tom asked.

"No. The ambulance officer said she must be in shock. Now we know what it takes to make her be quiet. I daresay she'll have a lot to say when she finally snaps out of it." She looked at the mangled remains of the vehicle. "If we'd delayed getting them out of the motor car…" She shook her head and looked away. "I can't imagine how she'll react when she eventually recovers from the shock." Evie only knew Isabel would be devastated…

"Well… If everyone is fine I think I shall be on my way," Sir Warwick said. "If I can be of any service, don't hesitate to contact me. Anyone in the village will be able to give you directions." He tipped his hat and went on his way.

Five minutes later, the police arrived and after inspecting the wreckage they asked for their statements.

Evie could feel Tom becoming impatient as the constable asked her the same questions he had asked Tom.

"Lady Woodridge has suffered a shock. I think we have provided enough information, constable. We would like to continue on our journey."

Evie glanced at him. Surely, he didn't think they would go on as if nothing had happened. "Is there a pub in the village?"

The constable nodded. "There is, my lady. The Pecking Goose."

"That's where we are meeting the rest of our party. Constable, if you have any further questions that is where you will find us."

They left the police to further investigate the accident site. Evie had several more sips of her cider before saying, "I simply cannot believe that just happened. What do you make of it all?"

Tom didn't answer straightaway. He drove at a sedate pace and appeared to be lost in his thoughts.

Eventually, he suggested, "I think there might have been something wrong with the driver."

"I agree. I could see Isabel trying to commandeer the vehicle. Do you think that's what made it swerve out of control?"

He tapped his finger on the steering wheel. "This

might be too much information for you but you saw what I saw. I had to wedge his foot out." He glanced at Evie. "I think Lorenzo died before the car crashed."

"Did you tell the police that?"

"No. It's all coming to me now. His foot appeared to be wedged between the accelerator and the brake pedal. We'll know more when Isabel recovers from the shock."

Evie spent the rest of the drive shaking her head in disbelief. To think Unique had wanted to become involved in a mystery. She'd be quite annoyed to hear what she'd missed.

Had Lorenzo had some sort of attack? He and Isabel must have set off early from London. How long had he been driving? What if he'd fallen asleep and Isabel hadn't been able to wake him up?

When the car had finally crashed, his body had been thrown forward and they'd found him slumped over the steering wheel.

It would be difficult to tell if he had already been dead before the crash. As Tom had said, they would have to wait for Isabel to recover from the experience.

Until then…

They could only guess.

Leaning back in her seat, Evie closed her eyes and tried to clear her mind.

Several minutes later, Tom said, "We're here."

Evie waited until the car came to a full stop before opening her eyes.

Glancing up and down the street, she saw several groups of people gathered at various points along the village street, all talking and gazing down the road.

News about the accident had evidently reached them.

"You should do all the talking," Evie said as they made their way toward the Pecking Goose. "They might smell cider on me and think we are on some sort of drinking binge."

"Glad to see you have recovered your sense of humor."

"It's only now coming back to me. I'm afraid I might be using it as a coping mechanism. Although, I should adopt a more somber attitude. I wouldn't want anyone to think I'm insensitive."

As they entered the pub, she looked over her shoulder. "I wonder how long it will take the others to arrive. I'm feeling rather guilty for running off as I did. What if this is all my fault. If I'd stayed on at the house, Isabel would not have given chase and Lorenzo would still be alive." Evie gasped and realized she was once again sounding like Isabel and talking a mile a minute. "I'm not sure I can deal with this guilt. Am I being selfish thinking about myself?"

Tom tugged her inside. "If you're going to talk through it, you should sit down first and have a proper drink."

"I don't hear you trying to dissuade me from feeling as I do."

"Would it work?"

Evie heard herself yelp, "We won't know until you try."

Chapter Seven

AN IMPROMPTU HOUSE PARTY

Two hours later, the Pecking Goose

*C*harlie, Lord Braithwaite, strode in, his hands in his pockets, his eyes dancing around as if searching for something to capture his attention.

Unique and Lord Alexander Saunders followed, their arms entwined, their lips stretched into bright smiles.

The others followed with Batty bringing up the rear.

Evie and Tom watched them with interest. They had sat down to lunch and had spent half an hour pushing their food around their plates. In the end, they had given up saying they had lost their appetites.

"They are either oblivious to what's happened or they are taking it all in their stride. Do you think the police have already cleared the wreckage from the roadside?"

"They must have," Tom said. "I don't see anyone looking particularly concerned."

Spotting Phillipa, Evie waved. "I think she might be able to tell us something," Evie murmured. "She's the only one in the group with a solemn expression."

Phillipa drew out a chair and removed the goggles she had hanging around her neck.

Evie exchanged a look with Tom. "You must have driven at great speeds to get here so quickly."

"Breakneck," Phillipa agreed. "It can be exhausting. We took turns to lead the group. We do that to stay alert."

"Did you see anything along the way?"

Phillipa nodded. "Near here." She looked up and gave a weary smile. "I'd kill for a cup of tea but I'll settle for a glass of ale."

"What did you see?"

"Oh, we didn't exactly see much of anything. There were a couple of police cars blocking the view and, despite slowing down, we were waved on. Do you know what happened?"

Oh, dear...

"Brace yourself." Evie took hold of Phillipa's hands. "I'm afraid I have some bad news." Before Evie could break the news, Unique screeched. Evie looked around and saw the young woman standing at the bar.

"W-what?" Unique screeched again.

The group huddled around Unique and talked at a rate of knots.

"I think they have just been informed."

"Of what?" Phillipa asked.

"Isabel Fitzpatrick and her husband, Lorenzo Bianchi, were involved in a car accident." Evie went on to explain how she'd bumped into her old friend in town and had then received a telegram informing her of their plans to drive down to Halton House.

Phillipa leaned forward, her eyes sparkling with interest. "Heavens. They arrived at Halton House soon after you left. When told of your departure, they decided to give chase. Are they all right?"

Before Evie could answer, the pub erupted in a wave of exclamations filled with disbelief. A couple of men staggered back and collapsed onto chairs. Questions were fired in every direction but no one had answers.

"What's going on?" Phillipa asked and half rose out of her chair.

"I'm afraid they are not quite all right… Lorenzo Bianchi died in the crash."

"But how?" Phillipa asked.

Tom gave an account of everything they had seen. "The police are investigating."

As if on cue, the constable strode into the pub. Looking around, he settled his gaze on Evie and Tom and made his way toward their table.

"I've been sent to ask if you could please remain in the vicinity. A detective will soon be arriving from London and he would like to speak with you."

"How long are we expected to remain here?" Evie asked, her tone carrying the weight of her title, something she rarely exploited. While she wished to be helpful, she also needed to return home. "It's already the middle of the afternoon." They couldn't travel at night and the sooner they got on their way, the sooner they could get back to Halton House.

"As long as it takes," the constable said.

"Are you saying we must simply bide our time here until the detective shows up?"

The constable nodded. Turning to Phillipa, he asked for her name. "And what is your association with Lady Woodridge?"

Evie spoke up, "She is my house guest."

"Were Isabel and Lorenzo Bianchi your house guests too?"

Evie turned to Tom and then shook her head. "No, but… they had stopped at Halton House to see me."

"Lady Woodridge, earlier you said you were meeting a group of people." The constable looked around the pub. "Are they with you too?"

When Evie nodded, he continued, "And were they guests at your house?"

"Well… Yes, but only for a night."

The constable wrote something down and said, "I expect the detective will want to speak with everyone."

Tom objected. "And what do you propose we do in the meantime?"

"This pub should be able to accommodate you."

Indeed, the pub couldn't accommodate them. The roof had suffered some damage the previous winter and the repairs were taking longer than anticipated.

"What does this mean?" Phillipa asked. "Why are the police investigating?"

Evie leaned forward and whispered, "Tom thinks Lorenzo might have died before the car crashed." Evie watched Phillipa as she processed the information. "If he's suspicious, then I imagine the police have entertained their own ideas. They would obviously have more experience with this type of accident." Turning to Tom, she asked, "Did you notice anything odd about Lorenzo?"

"Such as?" Tom asked.

"Something that might suggest he'd died before-hand." Evie gave a small shrug. "We've read enough books on the subject to know some poisons leave traces such as the scent of almonds."

"I only checked for a pulse." Tom straightened.

"What?"

"I need to stretch my legs."

"I'll join you. I think I could do with some fresh air." Patting Phillipa's hand, Evie said, "You look pale."

"I'm fine but I need more time for all this to sink in."

Evie caught the attention of a waiter and ordered some food and drink for Phillipa. Two others joined her table.

Evie looked at the man but drew a blank.

"It's Edward Spencer," Phillipa said. "And this is Marjorie."

Oh, yes…

Plain Marjorie who had something in common with Tom.

When a couple of others from the group joined them, including Lark Wainscot, Evie excused herself and went outside in search of Tom.

She found him by the village green sitting on a bench, his cap tipped back, his gaze fixed on a puffy cloud hovering above the village. He wore a different coat to the one he'd worn earlier and Evie assumed he had retrieved it from his luggage…

"Have you managed to clear your thoughts?" Evie asked.

Drawing in a deep breath, he leaned forward. "His lips were blue."

Evie sat down next to him. Biting the edge of her lip, she said, "If he'd died on impact his lips would still have looked normal. So, he must have died before. Is that what you're saying?"

He nodded.

Evie wondered how long it would take for lips to turn blue.

"I saw a man choke on a peanut once," Tom said. "He struggled to draw a breath and his lips turned blue quite quickly. He eventually recovered. Lorenzo might have had some sort of attack while driving."

"And you think that's when Isabel tried to take control of the vehicle."

"I assume that's what happened. He might have choked or… he might have had a heart attack."

When Evie had met Lorenzo Bianchi, he'd looked perfectly healthy. Tall with a strong physique, his eyes had been bright, his cheeks showing good health…

"How's Phillipa?" Tom asked. "Is she still in shock over the news?"

"Yes. I left her with…" she clicked her fingers, "the fellow with ginger hair, Edward Spencer and a couple of others. Let me think, Anthony Wright. Peter Berkley. Marjorie and… the woman with a bird name."

"Lark Wainscot."

"I take it you spoke with her too."

"I had a brief chat with her last night. She wants to become a stage actress."

"Not a film star?"

"No, she explained she is a purist, whatever that means."

They sat in silence for a while. Evie wished they could all go home and put this behind them. Then she thought about Isabel. She would need somewhere to stay while arrangements were made for the funeral.

So much for trying to avoid her...

When a couple of people emerged from the pub, Tom mused, "Charlie and Batty are both Lords. What does that mean... What sort of title is it?"

"It's difficult to say. It depends on their fathers and on whether they're first born or second born sons," Evie explained. "Sara would be able to tell you more about their parents but their fathers are most likely peers."

"And they stand to inherit."

"Yes. If they're first born sons."

"If they stand to inherit the title and everything that goes with it, shouldn't they be applying themselves to learning the ropes?"

"They're probably sowing their wild oats," Evie said.

"Or rebelling?"

Evie shrugged. "I doubt it. They're groomed from an early age to accept their responsibilities. Where are you going with this?"

"I'm trying to distract myself," Tom said.

Evie followed the direction of his gaze. Charlie and Batty stood outside the pub talking. "I suppose they needed to step out for a breath of air. Are you curious enough to want to know what they're talking about?"

"I imagine they are making plans for the night."

"That would be too practical for them. Perhaps they sabotaged Lorenzo Bianchi's car and are now getting their story straight."

Tom glanced at her. "Are you just making conversation or are you being serious?"

"Like you, I am trying to distract myself. In any case, here's something else to take your mind off. Since the pub can't accommodate us, we need to find somewhere else to spend the night." With the greatest reluctance, Evie drew out the list Sara had provided. "Sir Warwick is on it."

"I'm not surprised," Tom said. "After all, he claims to know Lady Sara."

Glancing at the list, Evie said, "Sara knows a great number of people. I suppose I do too. But no one in the immediate vicinity." Huffing out a breath, she added, "The constable should not have asked us to remain here. We can't be expected to impose on the local gentry at a moment's notice."

She looked across the street at Charlie and Batty. "They look relaxed." As if they were conversing about nothing more mundane than the weather, she thought.

"Batty rubbed his neck a couple of times. That's a sign of concern about something." Tom straightened. "What does his lordship who stands to inherit a title worry about?"

"In my experience? He is likely to be concerned about what he'll wear to this year's Derby." She looked away and turned slightly to gaze down the road. "The police wish to speak with us and with our car rally companions. What does that mean? We've already provided them with all the information we have."

"If I had to guess," Tom said, "the police are interested in what happened before and after Isabel and Lorenzo left Halton House."

Evie brushed her fingers across her eyes. "I suppose we should ask for directions to Sir Warwick's house."

"No need. There he is," Tom said and drew her attention back to the pub.

"Where did he come from?"

Tom leaned slightly to gaze down the side street. "I think that's his motor car. He must have been in the village all along."

And now Charlie and Batty had engaged him in conversation.

"He's looking this way."

"Should I wave?" Evie asked. "I get the feeling Charlie and Batty mentioned me and that's why he looked at us."

Sir Warwick tipped his hat.

"That's your cue and invitation to seek refuge with him," Tom said. "As the highest-ranking member of our group, you alone stand a chance of securing us a roof over our heads for the night."

"Us? It might be time to cut everyone loose and look after my own interests."

Tom grinned. "And how will you get home?"

"Oh, that's right. Fine, I suppose I can get you in and… and Phillipa too."

"You're in luck. He is coming to you."

Sir Warwick tipped his hat. "We meet again, Lady Woodridge. And I see there is no happy conclusion to your tale. I should like to extend an invitation to you and your fellow travelers."

Tom nudged Evie.

"Sir Warwick. It is very kind of you to offer. You have spared me the embarrassment of having to ask. The police have put us in an impossible situation."

"Yes, those young fellows have just been telling me. Well, you are in luck. Warwick Hall is at your disposal."

He proceeded to give them directions saying he would hurry back to make the arrangements.

"And you didn't even have to ask," Tom mused.

"Are you trying to make a point?"

"Only that a regular person would have to sleep on a park bench while you have access to a manor house."

"I refuse to apologize for my privileged status. For your information, I am not even embarrassed by all the advantages I enjoy." Glancing at him, she saw his lips lifted into a smile. "You're teasing me."

"And you are so easy to tease."

Chapter Eight

EVERY MAN IS GUILTY OF ALL THE GOOD HE DID NOT
DO - VOLTAIRE

*A*s they made their way to Sir Richard Warwick's home, Evie tried to sit back in silent introspection but there were too many thoughts colliding in her mind. So, she prattled on, "Queen Elizabeth used to travel around a great deal, staying in the great houses at no cost to herself. If I put my mind to it, I could spend the better part of the year as a guest."

"Are you still trying to distract yourself?" Tom asked.

"Partly." No matter what she thought about, the feeling of guilt kept surging inside her.

If she hadn't been such a coward, she would have stayed at Halton House and welcomed Isabel...

Evie shook the thought away and focused on the road ahead. "I'm afraid I'm not really succeeding since I am now obsessing about barging in on an unsuspecting soul. Poor Sir Richard doesn't know what he's in for."

"He invited you."

"That's beside the point. I'm sure he felt obligated to offer me shelter. Anyhow, as I was saying, others before me have made a habit of being a guest."

Tom laughed. "You want to spend your life on the run, making a nuisance of yourself?"

"Yes, but what would I do with you? If I introduced you as my bodyguard, I would become the laughing stock in all the counties in England. Evangeline Halton, Countess of Woodridge, thinks herself a cut above everyone." Also, it would seem odd to travel with someone intent on keeping her safe. Although… gentlemen traveled with their valets and titled ladies were invariably accompanied by their maids.

"Considering how cash poor some of the landed gentry seem to be these days, they would be right to think you're acting all superior."

"Speaking of which… Sort of. I think the dowagers are dispossessing me from the inside out."

"Pardon?"

"Caro told me they raided the attics and took away quite a few pieces of furniture."

"Did you ask them about it?"

"Of course not. You know as well as I do, there is simply no point in asking outright what they are up to."

"But it doesn't stop you from forming your own suspicions. What makes you think they would want to, as you say, dispossess you?"

"Even after all these years, I still feel somewhat of an outsider. They were both mistresses of Halton House and now they are living in the dower house. Some might view that as a step down." As the Countess of Woodridge, Evie retained the right to live at Halton House. However, if she were to marry again…

Evie tilted her head. She had never given it any thought because it almost went without saying, she would never marry again. Recently, Henrietta had told her it would be perfectly normal for Evie to want to move on. In any case, if she did marry again, she would lose her title and Halton House.

How did she feel about that?

Tom frowned. "You think they resent you?"

"That's probably going too far," Evie said.

"What if they are only trying to make use of furniture that would otherwise take up space in the attic? It must get very dusty there."

"The dower house is already crammed full of odds and ends." Evie tapped her chin in thought. "They both have their own money and also receive an adequate amount from the estate to cover living expenses but what if it's not enough and they are now trying to raise funds by selling valuable furniture? I've heard some peers are reduced to disposing of art works and such to pay for the upkeep of their large estates."

Tom laughed. "You might want to take inventory or put new locks on the doors at Halton House. Although, it might be too late. Who knows what awaits you on your return. They might have cleaned you out."

Evie closed her eyes and entertained the thought. Would the staff go about their business as if nothing had happened? Caro had said the footmen had been employed to load up the furniture. She got on well with her staff but she might have missed signs of dissent and… dissatisfaction. Her staff could be aiding and abetting the dowagers…

"What can the dowagers be getting up to?" Evie whispered. She imagined Henrietta defending her actions by saying she only had Evie's best interest at heart. "I suppose I'll find out soon enough."

Turning, she checked on the roadsters behind them.

Tom had requested they all drive at a sedate pace. Evie thought she'd also heard him issuing instructions to be on their best behavior.

"I do hope they remember their manners." Evie gasped and straightened. "I have been so overwhelmed by the accident and preoccupied with the aftermath, I forgot about our flat tire. We need to find out who is responsible. Do you have any ideas?"

"Not really."

"I think we should try to find out if there is a prankster among them. Phillipa should be able to help us out."

"Who made the suggestion we drive out ahead of everyone?" Tom asked.

"That would be Sara. Then Charlie jumped onboard with the idea. Remember, we thought there might be a wager involved." And that, Evie thought, would give Charlie motive to drive a nail through their tire to slow them down. Would he do something so reckless?

Evie gasped and pressed her hand against her mouth.

"What?" Tom asked.

She couldn't say it.

What if Sara... No. Impossible.

Although, she had been the one to suggest they leave ahead of everyone else.

"I think the dowagers might be trying to kill me."

Tom tipped his head back and laughed. "Are you trying to lighten the mood?"

"Yes, I suppose I am. Is there any chance you might have driven over a nail?"

"It's possible," Tom said.

But highly unlikely, Evie thought.

"That must be the house up ahead," Tom said.

"Oh my… It's more imposing than I imagined it would be." Warwick Hall sat on a slight slope with a lush green lawn stretching out before it. The Jacobean style house had columns with elaborate carvings, pilasters and round-arch arcades. Admiring the turrets and mullioned windows, Evie changed her mind and thought it had a touch of Elizabethan architecture.

Sir Richard Warwick welcomed everyone and showed them through to a high-ceilinged drawing room decorated with coats of arms.

"There have been many knights in our family going back to William the Conqueror. One of them was gifted this land and house for his chivalry on the battle field. I always think I must be a disappointment to my ancestors. I can shoot but I would not be able to wield a sword to save my life. Also, a bad heart prevented me from serving." Smiling, he clasped his hands and rubbed them together. "The household is thrilled to have such a large party. They haven't seen this many people in over a year."

Evie hesitated. She didn't feel comfortable asking for details and, thankfully, she didn't have to.

"My wife passed on and I'm afraid I haven't been very good company. I have two sons but they have both traveled abroad to seek their fortunes."

Offering her condolences for the loss of his wife, Evie then asked, "I presume one of your sons will return to take over from you when the time comes."

"Oh, yes. Absolutely. But he's in no hurry. At the moment, he's intent on learning as much as he can about the banking industry. My other son has a keen interest in agriculture. At times, I think they have conspired to make me incredibly proud of them."

Evie sensed a few of the bright young things shifting and clearing their throats. In their place, she would feel uncomfortable knowing others were taking such grown-up steps to ensure they would contribute to the upkeep of their inheritance as well as to the next generation.

"I suppose you should all like to change for dinner," Sir Richard said. "My butler, Wilson, will show you through to your rooms."

They all strode up the intricately carved staircase stopping along the way to admire the armors on display.

"These must have cost a pretty penny in their time," Evie mused. "We have several on display and some are in the attic."

Tom chuckled. "I just pictured Lady Henrietta absconding with one."

"We shouldn't laugh. What if they have developed some sort of affliction?"

"Such as?"

"Kleptomania." Evie shuddered. "Heavens, I said it in jest but now I have to wonder. I've been expanding my reading and I came across a book citing a couple of French psychiatrists." Glancing at Tom, she saw his eyebrows quirk up. "Yes, I am still continuing with my study of Sigmund Freud. Anyhow, from memory, klepto-mania is a type of impulse control disorder. Sufferers of this affliction steal items of trivial value and then feel dreadfully guilty about it."

"And you think both dowagers suffer from this affliction?"

"It seems unlikely. Perhaps they are only playing with me." But why? Did they need to draw attention to themselves? Reaching the landing, Evie stopped. "I think I have just found another reason to feel guilty. I should be home taking care of them. This could be their cry for help. And here I am, galivanting around the countryside."

Cupping her elbow and leading Evie up the stairs, Tom asked, "What are the symptoms?"

"Symptoms? Of my guilt or their kleptomania? My shoulders are rather tense…so my guilt is still plaguing me. As for the kleptomania. Let's see, there's a feeling of pleasure, relief or gratification while stealing. I can imagine they must have had fun going up to the attics while I was away in town. I actually asked Henrietta about one of the items she took. A vase. She had it on display in her drawing room."

"And?"

"She dismissed it with a wave of her hand and said it had been in the family for a long time. She also expressed surprise because I hadn't noticed it before… or because I had noticed it." Evie gasped. "She lied to me."

"And what do your books say about that?"

"Henrietta is flaunting her act of rebellion in my face. Oh, heavens. And now, I've left Sara in charge of the house and she's the one who encouraged us to join the car rally group. She wanted me out of the house… Who knows what I'll be going back to…"

The butler, Wilson, gestured to the right of the hall-way. "This is your room, Lady Woodridge, and Mr. Winchester is across the hall. I hope that is satisfactory."

Without giving it much thought, Evie nodded. She strode into her room and removed her coat. Setting it down, she explored the elegantly appointed room with its four-poster bed and views of the surrounding countryside.

The maid must have been busy while Sir Richard had entertained them in the drawing room.

Her clothes had been unpacked and a light green evening dress spread out on the bed. Nudging a door open, she sighed with relief when she saw a boudoir complete with bathtub. What she wouldn't give to sink into a comforting bath, but it would have to wait until tomorrow.

A light knock at the door preceded the maid's entrance. She introduced herself as Pearl. "I'll be assisting you this evening."

"Oh, marvelous. I thought I would have to manage by myself." Not that it would have been a problem, Evie thought, since Caro had chosen the gowns which required the least assistance. "Sir Richard said he'd been widowed for a year. Does he still keep a full complement of staff?"

"He does indeed, milady. He doesn't have the heart to let anyone go. And he keeps wanting to get back into the swing of things but, these days, he tends to keep to himself in the library. We're all very excited about your visit…"

Evie's guilt over Isabel's accident lifted ever so slightly. Although, now she couldn't help seeing herself as a source of amusement and entertainment.

Caro had told her the staff always looked forward to house parties with great anticipation as the guests tended to provide them with amusing tales.

"We heard about the accident, milady. Did you witness it?"

Evie shuddered. "I did." In that brief second, her

mind filled with images of the roadster careening toward her. What if it had swerved the other way? "A close call," she mused.

"Did you know the driver?"

"I met him briefly and… I know his wife." Evie sat down on the edge of the bed.

They had visited the hospital and had tried to see Isabel but the doctor had given her something to make her sleep. As soon as the detective arrived and she answered all his questions, she would ask Tom to drive to the hospital again. Isabel would need someone familiar around her and....

"Oh, heavens."

"Is everything all right, milady?"

Evie looked up. "Oh, yes. I just remembered something." Or, rather, something had just occurred to her. Isabel would need time to heal and a place to do it in...

She couldn't see any way around it.

Isabel would have to recuperate at Halton House.

Chapter Nine

ALWAYS THANK YOUR HOST TWICE - EMILY POST

The dining room, Warwick Hall

$\mathcal{E}$vie raised her glass of wine. "My compliments to your cook. It could not have been easy to put together a delectable meal at such short notice, Sir Richard."

"Oh, please call me Richard. These days, peers are either allowing such formalities to lapse or holding on to them with a death grip as everything else crumbles around them. I say we need to move on and keep up with the times."

For someone who kept to himself, Sir Richard certainly had a lot to say. Evie had the feeling he wouldn't be a widower for much longer. His affable manner alone would be enough to attract someone new into his life. His distinguished good looks would also help...

"I hope you have all found your quarters acceptable."

Everyone expressed their gratitude and offered assurances. As Evie sat back to allow a footman to clear her plate, she remembered what the butler had said to her.

After he'd directed Tom to the room opposite Evie's, he'd said he'd hoped that would be satisfactory. Why wouldn't it be? Leaning slightly forward, Evie glanced at Tom. He sat next to Marjorie at the other end of the table. After watching him for several minutes, she noticed their conversation flowed with ease.

Nothing wrong with his affability either, Evie thought.

Glancing around the dining room, she saw the butler casting his keen eye over the table.

Evie's thoughts returned to the butler's earlier remark… Had he meant to imply she was having some sort of liaison with Tom?

House parties were notorious for such goings on. Not that she had ever partaken of the activity…

As she returned her attention to her meal, she saw the butler approach Sir Richard. A moment later, Sir Richard cleared his throat and excused himself.

"I wonder what that's about?" Batty asked.

An unexpected visitor, Evie thought. In her experience, butlers did not interrupt for any other reason. Not even if there was a fire in the kitchen. And the host would certainly never leave the table unless he absolutely had to, and only because no one else could attend to a matter...

Taking a sip of her wine, she exchanged a few raised

eyebrow gestures with Phillipa who sat across the table from her.

Wearing a black and white striped dress, her young friend looked surprisingly staid. She even wore a head-band adorned with a black feather. Unique sat two places down from her. She had stayed in character, wearing a man's coattails with a wide belt and some sort of skirt underneath.

Sir Richard's return to the dining room drew everyone's attention to him.

"It would seem we have an extra guest," Batty murmured.

Stepping aside, Sir Richard gestured to a man who stood at the door. "This is Detective Inspector O'Neill from Scotland Yard."

The butler jumped into action setting a dinner place at the table for the detective… right next to Evie.

"Lady Woodridge."

Evie inclined her head. "Detective. I want to say it is lovely to meet you again, but the circumstances make it rather awkward."

"Indeed."

Evie smiled. "Please say you are surprised to find me here."

The detective settled into his chair. "When Sir Richard mentioned you were one of the guests, I must admit I felt surprise at the coincidence. And, as you well know, I'm not overly fond of coincidences. However, given the circumstances, I believe this can work in our favor. You already know what to expect and I hope to be able to secure your assistance."

High praise indeed, Evie thought. "I must say, I am surprised a Scotland Yard detective has traveled all this way. Surely this is only a car accident. Something that could be dealt with by the local constabulary."

"And yet here I am."

"Which begs the question…"

"I believe you are acquainted with Mrs. Bianchi," he said.

Evie explained her friendship with Isabel, leaving out most of her personal opinions about the relationship, something the detective had no trouble picking up on.

"I sense there is much you are leaving out."

"I'll be happy to answer any of your questions, detective." And hope that he would in turn answer some of her questions. Why had a Scotland Yard detective been sent to investigate a motor car accident? Why had he asked about Isabel? Did Isabel's prominent family have something to do with his involvement?

They would have been informed of the accident and she wouldn't be surprised if the Ambassador himself had become involved, ensuring the matter received the utmost attention.

He glanced around the table. "This is quite an interesting… Well… words fail me."

"Menagerie?" Evie suggested. "They are all rather colorful and somewhat wild."

"I would have settled for group of people but menagerie describes them perfectly. Friends of yours?" he asked.

How could she answer that?

"Well… they landed on my doorstep and I couldn't turn them away."

"Did you try?"

Smiling, she nodded. "I would have but they were looking for Phillipa Brady. You remember Phillipa."

"Yes, how could I forget. Does she still believe Scotland Yard is in Scotland?"

"No, we have managed to set her straight." When Evie told the inspector about Phillipa getting lost, he laughed.

"Does she not know north from south?"

"I'm sure she does, but she is from Australia and from what she tells us everything appears to be on the reverse side down there."

"You jest."

"Yes, of course." She hadn't had the opportunity to ask how Phillipa had managed to get lost, but she suspected it had something to do with being sidetracked. Keeping her voice lowered to a murmur, Evie pointed out the other guests and shared her limited knowledge of them.

"It still amazes me how some people can go about their lives as if they haven't a care in the world," the detective observed.

Evie waited for him to relate some sort of tale about his youth and how he'd had to carry out chores from dusk to dawn until his nineteenth birthday when he'd finally been allowed to further his studies.

"May I ask why you are investigating a car accident?"

He gave it some thought and to Evie's surprise he actually answered.

"It might not have been an accident."

Evie lowered her tone to barely a whisper. "You suspect foul play?"

He gave a small nod.

"Did someone alert you to the possibility?" She thought Isabel's family might have pushed to have the incident thoroughly investigated. She simply couldn't see any other reason for a Scotland Yard detective being sent down...

"Yes, and that is all I am prepared to say at the moment."

Heavens. He'd obviously made a concession for her. Several, in fact. But he had limits and boundaries.

Looking down the table, she saw Tom still immersed in his conversation with 'plain' Marjorie. She couldn't wait to share the news.

"So, tell me about this car rally you're involved in," the detective encouraged.

"Oh... I'm afraid it's nothing more than a yearning for adventure. A spur of the moment decision."

"You were bored?" he asked.

"Does it sound so out of character?" Evie asked even as she wondered if she should take care how she answered his questions. At this stage, she had no clear idea of what he might be investigating.

"Well, last time I saw you, you were in the midst of organizing a major event at Halton House."

True. The Hunt Ball.

"It has been temporarily postponed until further notice."

"I'm sorry to hear that. Did the decision have anything to do with the incidents that took place at Halton?"

"Yes, in the end, the dowagers agreed we needed to let the dust settle before going ahead with the Hunt Ball." Two prominent members of the community had died while in the process of planning the ball. They had all decided it would be in poor taste to proceed with the event so soon after their deaths. Evie had been rather pleased with the dowagers for reaching such a sensible decision.

Also, as she still felt the two years she had been abroad had left a gap, she thought the extra time would give her the opportunity to settle into the district before holding the major event.

"You said you met your friend, Isabel Bianchi, in town."

"Yes. It's strange to hear you refer to her by that name. I've always known her as Fitzpatrick. Now I assume she will revert to her maiden name."

"What do you know of her current circumstances?"

"Apart from her marriage? She said she traveled a great deal with her husband. He is… was a racing car driver."

"Yes, I've heard of him. I suppose I meant to ask about her financial situation."

"Detective, I'm shocked. You know as well as I do, no one likes to talk about money."

"No one in England," he said. "But you're American."

"As the saying goes, when in Rome…"

"Oh, I assumed you wanted to assist with my investigation."

Evie drew in a breath. "Since you put it that way… The Fitzpatrick family are among the four hundred in New York." Evie took pleasure in explaining in great detail how only four hundred people could fit into Mrs. Astor's ballroom. Half way through, she thought she detected his eyes glazing over and then she remembered she had already imparted the information during their last encounter.

"In other words, they are extremely wealthy."

Evie nodded. "If their circumstances had changed, I can assure you someone would have let me know. It's just the sort of information either my mother or grandmother would share in a letter."

Did he want to know if Isabel faced financial difficulties? And, if so, what would it have to do with the car accident?

"What about her husband? What do you know about him?"

"I only met him briefly." And that had been enough for Evie. "He talked at great length about cars and nothing else. Oh, wait. I also recall some mention about wine. I believe he originally hailed from Tuscany. Do you want to know if he appeared to be solvent?" Evie didn't wait for the detective to respond. "Hard to say. He might have been living off Isabel's fortune or maybe he had his own money. They were staying at the Automobile Club in London. You could make inquiries." Evie raised her glass only to set it down again.

"You just thought of something," the detective said.

"How well you seem to know me." She gave him a brisk smile. "As a matter of fact, yes. I remember Isabel saying she had come to England to seek fame and fortune." An odd remark, Evie thought. "She already has access to a significant fortune."

The detective shrugged. "For some people, a lot is never enough."

As the footmen served the next course, Evie pondered the possibility of Isabel needing to access more funds. How would she do that? Were they hoping to win a race? "Is there much money involved in motor car racing?"

"More and more every day. It makes me think I am in the wrong profession." Looking down at his dessert, he smiled. "I suppose the grass is always greener no matter where I look."

She picked up her glass again and this time, she focused on enjoying her drink only to sigh.

"Have you thought of something else?" the detective asked, his tone sounding slightly surprised.

Evie looked around and tried to catch the attention of a footman. Suddenly, she needed another drink.

"Something else Isabel said might or might not be useful. It's connected to her other remark. She felt there were plenty of people willing to do anything for money. Of course, I'm taking it all out of context but sometimes we talk about things that take up space in our minds."

Could money be connected to Lorenzo Bianchi's death?

Chapter Ten

THE ROOT OF ALL EVIL

Warwick Hall library

*E*vie felt obliged to again say, "Richard, you have been so wonderfully accommodating. I feel dreadful for imposing on you."

"Nonsense. It's not the first time I have offered shelter to a traveler and it won't be the last, I'm sure." He stirred his coffee. "Have the police provided more information? I couldn't help noticing you were deep in conversation with the detective. You know, he specifically asked to be seated next to you."

"He and I have met before."

"Is that so?" He looked up. "Oh, wait. Yes… I did hear something. Or maybe I read it. I get all the daily newspapers. Even some from abroad. Feel free to use the library."

"I daresay, we should be out of your hair in no time. I doubt I'll be here long enough to enjoy more than a brisk glance at the daily news. The detective's investigation shouldn't take too long. He only wants to interview everyone while they are all here."

Sir Richard mused, "It makes you wonder…"

Evie mentally filled in the gap by thinking there might be a killer among them. She stilled and chastised herself for considering such a silly idea.

A wealthy family wanted answers because their daughter had been involved in a near fatal accident, one which had killed her husband. She shouldn't read more into it…

"What's that?" she asked Sir Richard.

"Oh, well… From what I understand, everyone here had been at your house and the car accident victim had also been at your house."

Oh, please, don't say it, she silently begged. It had been bad enough to entertain the idea in her mind…

"For all we know, there might be a killer among us and it could all have started at Halton House."

Evie glanced around the library and found Tom standing by the window gazing out. He had not been pleased about the arrangements, but Detective Inspector O'Neill had insisted they all needed to stay together until the matter could be fully investigated.

What did that even mean?

Were they to take up permanent residence at Sir Richard's manor house?

The detective hadn't provided any solid information. He had suggested someone had pushed for an investigation, but he hadn't named the person.

The clock on the mantelpiece struck the hour. Dinner had been a somber affair, mostly because no one had wanted to talk about the death and, Evie imagined, they probably thought tackling any other subject would be in poor taste.

Sir Richard had done his best to ensure the conversation flowed by showing an interest in his guests where none could possibly exist. A scholar, he had been speechless at first, his eyes almost popping out of their sockets at the sight of the colorful group as they had all chosen to wear the most flamboyant ensembles, but he had adjusted. Just as well the bright young things' usual behavior hadn't matched their outrageous clothes.

When their host had excused himself saying he had an early start to the day and encouraged them to stay on, everyone had settled in for a long night but no one had wanted to talk about what had happened.

They would have to… eventually.

Detective Inspector O'Neill stood at the end of the library perusing the contents of a bookcase. However, Evie suspected his attention remained focused on the group.

"What are you scribbling, Charlie?" Unique asked.

"I'm jotting down some ideas."

"For the book you keep saying you will eventually, someday soon, or in the near future, whenever that might be, start to write?"

Charlie grinned. "That's the one."

"Tell us what you have," Unique encouraged. "We might be able to give you the push you so obviously need."

Charlie stretched his legs out. "I've been thinking

about writing a story about the stories people wish to write."

Unique pulled up a footstool and sat at his feet. "I'm intrigued but it sounds as if you wish to become a ghost writer."

"You miss the point. I've come across many people who say they plan on writing a book someday because they feel they have a story in them. So, my hero…"

"Why does it always have to be a hero? Why not a female lead?" Unique complained.

"I would indulge you, but in this case the hero needs to be free to travel around and, let's face it, women have been shackled. Yes, some do travel but there are restrictions. Anyhow, my hero travels around the country listening to people's stories…"

Evie searched for Tom. He had moved away from the window and had now settled by a bookcase. She watched him for several minutes and, when she saw he hadn't turned the page of the book he held, she decided he was only pretending to read.

"Lady Woodridge."

Evie considered correcting Charlie and inviting him to call her Evie, but then she changed her mind. After all, someone had to be the grown-up.

"Do you have a story you think you will write someday?"

"No, I can't say that I do."

"Surely, you must."

Evie smiled. "Insisting will do you no good. I have never aspired to become a writer."

Charlie leaned forward. "But if you were to write a story, what would you write about?"

Did she really wish to play this game? A man had died. It almost felt disrespectful.

Setting the wine glass she had been nursing down on a side table, Evie surged to her feet and moved about the library inspecting the knickknacks on display. "I think I would want to write something significant and... definitely something different."

Unique snorted. "Such as a study of the rotational influences of the moon on the earth and all its inhabitants?"

Evie stopped in the middle of the room and tapped her chin. "No, I'm thinking more along the lines of Mary Shelley's Frankenstein or... Jules Verne's Journey to the Center of the Earth. So, I suppose I would also want to write something entertaining. Both books were written in the last century and they are still quite popular. The same can't be said for many of these tomes taking up space in this library. I'm sure they served their purpose at one time or other, but I doubt they entertained more than a handful of readers."

"Brava," Lord Saunders exclaimed. "I think it's a marvelous idea."

Evie turned to smile at him.

Alexander, Lord Saunders, had once again favored tartan, donning a black coattail jacket with tartan trousers.

Evie remembered Sir Richard's remark. Had something happened at Halton House? Did the car rally group have something to do with it? Her gaze skipped from one member to the other. They were all looking right back at her.

Resuming her stroll around the library, Evie turned and saw Tom had set his book down.

Even when her gaze met his, he didn't look away.

Had she engaged his interest?

Turning her attention back to the other guests, she realized they continued to chime in their responses to her answer.

"Well said, Countess. I dare say, I would love to see my books outlive me." Charlie sat up. "So, what type of story would you tell?"

Evie laughed. "I'm sure I have exhausted all my ideas for tonight."

"I somehow doubt it," Charlie said.

Strangely, Evie thought she heard Tom murmur the same remark.

"Give it your best shot," Unique encouraged.

Evie tipped her head to the side. "I wouldn't know where to begin."

Charlie urged her to ad lib.

She laughed. "I really would need more time. Phillipa wishes to write books. Maybe she can play this game."

Phillipa yawned. "The Lady Woodridge Mysteries. The story would open with you expounding on the benefits of a quiet life in the country where nothing much ever happens and then someone would turn up dead and you would solve the mystery. I'm sure you'll insist I use another name. I'll have to think of one."

"Your books could be serialized in ladies' magazines," Charlie suggested.

Unique laughed. "Now you'll have to write them, Phillipa. We'll badger you until you do."

When they all turned to Evie, she suspected they would harass her until she spun them a tale.

Crossing her arms, she struck up a pensive pose.

After a few moments of quiet deliberation, she said, "I think my story would be a mystery too but it would involve time travel." She looked up and saw everyone shifting and straightening. Evidently, she now had a captive audience.

Evie cleared her throat. "Investigating the murder of a mad scientist, the lady detective uses the scientist's latest invention to accidentally transport herself to the past where she comes face to face with a killer." Evie held up a finger as if calling for a moment. "Wait... I think it will be better if she travels to the future instead where she meets the reincarnated version of herself. So, when she realizes she has met her future reincarnated self, the killer, who has traveled to the past to kill the scientist, she returns to her time and tries to make sure she never makes the decision that will eventually turn her into a killer." Evie nibbled the tip of her finger. "Clearly, I would need to iron out the kinks."

Not knowing what sort of reaction to expect from her listeners, Evie gave a tentative smile.

Erupting to his feet, Charlie exclaimed, "Fabulous. How did you come up with that?"

Evie gestured to Phillipa. "I remembered Phillipa mentioned reincarnation recently. I suppose the moral of the story is to be careful what you do now because you might end up paying for it throughout eternity."

Everyone fell silent.

Out of guilt?

Could someone in the group really be responsible for Lorenzo's death?

Evie strode across the library and sat down next to Tom. "Well, do I have a decent story in me?"

"I think you do. I will look forward to reading it."

Evie laughed. "Does the world need another writer?"

"It does if the writer has an entertaining story to tell."

"I heard say you should write what you know." Evie glanced over at Phillipa. "If I were to set pen to paper, I would write about murder and mayhem in the countryside."

"If?"

"Sorry to disappoint. I have the Hunt Ball to plan as well as other events. That should keep me busy for a while." Remembering she had some news to share with Tom, she checked to make sure no one would hear her and lowered her voice to say, "It seems someone is putting pressure on the police to investigate the accident, which might not have been an accident after all."

"Has the detective shared his tactics with you?" Tom asked. "He appears to be taking it all in his stride."

"He's trying to put us all on edge, that's my guess. He could be trying to play us off against each other in the hope one of us will break and reveal all."

Tom lifted his whisky tumbler in a salute. "Your theory relies on one of us or all of us knowing something."

What if they did and didn't realize it? "Sir Richard made a valid observation," she said. "Isabel and Lorenzo first went to Halton House where they met with the car rally group. Then they drove out and… something happened to Lorenzo. He thinks all this started at Halton House."

Tom shifted in his chair. "I'd like to have an easy sleep. There's really nothing we can do without first knowing how Lorenzo died."

"You're right." And yet, Evie didn't feel at ease. They had both already suspected something had happened to Lorenzo before the car had crashed…

Evie cast her gaze around the library. Were they about to spend the night under the same roof as a killer?

Chapter Eleven

IN THE DEAD OF NIGHT

*H*earing a light tap on her bedroom door, Evie nudged it open a fraction.

"It's me. Phillipa."

"Come in," Evie whispered.

"You should not have opened the door."

"But you tapped on it."

"Yes, but… You didn't know who is was until I announced myself. Never mind… No one saw me so you shouldn't worry about people reaching the wrong conclusions."

Laughing lightly, Evie said, "Why am I suddenly picturing everyone with their ears pressed to their bedroom doors?"

"It's your vivid imagination." Phillipa settled down on the edge of the bed. "I can't sleep."

"No, nor can I. I would ring for some tea but I'm afraid that will raise the alarm. In reality, I wouldn't want to wake someone up just so I can indulge in a cup of tea." Evie sat at the other end of the bed. "Something has been bothering me a great deal. Did you see Isabel and Lorenzo's arrival at Halton House?"

Phillipa nodded. "I had just been making my way down the stairs when I saw Edgar showing them through to the drawing room. Once the others told them you had left, Isabel swung around and told her husband they had to catch up with you. She sounded determined."

"Yes, that sounds like Isabel. So, let me guess... They left straightaway."

"No. Lorenzo Bianchi insisted they needed to have a brief rest and some refreshments after their long drive." Phillipa got up and strode around the room. "They stayed for approximately half an hour. Isabel refused to sit still."

"But they had refreshments."

"Yes. Edgar brought in some tea and coffee."

"Did Lorenzo talk to anyone in particular?" Evie asked.

Phillipa gave it some thought. "We were all intrigued by the couple. Charlie and Unique fired one question after the other."

Evie tried to engage her imagination only to realize Tom had made a solid point. They needed to know how Lorenzo had died. Until then, they could only employ guesswork. However, she decided it shouldn't stop her from getting some sort of background information...

"Did anyone in the group actually know Lorenzo?"

"I don't think so. I strode into the drawing room just as Lorenzo was introducing himself to everyone."

"Do you remember if he had a private word with anyone?"

Phillipa stood still and gazed at her. "Do you have a theory taking shape in your mind?"

"No." Evie sighed. "I'm trying to paint a picture. Luckily, I don't have to try very hard because you were there."

Pressing her hands against her cheeks, Phillipa closed her eyes. "Let me think."

Evie strode to the dresser and searched through one of the drawers. When she didn't find what she wanted, she continued her search until the last drawer yielded some paper and a fountain pen.

When Phillipa opened her eyes, she found Evie sitting at the dresser.

"Are you going to take notes?"

"I'd like to place everyone. Can you remember where you were standing?"

"By the piano. That was the closest place to the door I could find to sit down. You know how it is when you are the last to arrive somewhere... Well, perhaps you don't. I tend to hover in the background trying to pick up the vibes in the place. I guess that makes me an intro-vert of sorts. Although, you wouldn't know it by looking at me. Anyhow, Isabel and Lorenzo sat by the fireplace."

"Together or opposite each other?"

"Together."

"And who sat opposite them?"

Phillipa gave a firm nod. "Unique and Marjorie." She closed her eyes again. "Charlie stood on the other side of the sofa between them. At one point, he leaned down and pressed his chin against the headrest. I remember thinking how odd it looked. You know, almost as if he didn't have a body."

"What about Batty?"

Phillipa smiled. "You seem to have become acquainted with everyone."

"He insisted I call him Batty. Now that I think about it, I meant to ask how he acquired the name."

"Oh, he enjoys playing cricket and is quite a good batsman. Apparently, he made his way through Oxford by hiring himself out as a batsman for struggling teams."

Evie had been about to say something else but Phillipa's remark lingered in her mind. "Pardon?"

"He supported himself by playing cricket."

She remembered Isabel saying some people were prepared to do anything for money. "He is Lord Hemsworth, and he attended Oxford. How could he possibly be in need of money?"

Phillipa inspected her nails. "I've heard whispers about his family keeping up appearances."

"So, they're having financial difficulties."

"Oh, it's been going on for some time. The Hemsworth estate is crumbling around them. Apparently, they only use the downstairs rooms because the upstairs ones are in a state of dereliction and they simply cannot afford to fix them."

Evie strode to the window and drew the thick velvet curtains open. She looked out at the clear indigo blue sky sparkling with stars. "How old is he?"

"Batty? He's about twenty-eight."

"He needs to find himself an heiress."

Phillipa snorted. "First, he needs to grow up. Batty appears to be in denial. You must think I have double standards because I'm running around with his crowd. Don't get me wrong, I love the freedom to come and go as I please and I'm sure he does too. But there's a big difference between us. I'm aware of the fact I need to make my own way in the world. No one will hand me an estate to live in. Yes, I received a small inheritance, but I think I'm putting it to good use."

Evie smiled but refrained from commenting.

Out of the corner of her eye, she saw Phillipa leaning forward as if trying to catch her expression.

"Yes, sorry… I am smiling. I may be an heiress but I know the average person would consider using the money to learn a trade rather than pursuing what they might think of as a whimsical dream."

Lifting her chin, Phillipa said, "Yes, I suppose you're right. That's precisely what I'm doing… more or less." She smiled. "I told you. I want to gain some life experience so I can then write about it. I'm sure I'll be able to earn a living out of it."

"I have no doubt you'll put your inheritance to good use. However, if you are serious about writing those mysteries, please do change the name of the protagonist. Remember, I am trying to lead a quiet life. Notoriety wouldn't suit the Countess of Woodridge."

"A quiet life?" Phillipa laughed. "I believe your destiny has already been chosen. You no longer have a say in the matter. In fact, I might take up Tom's suggestion and write your memoirs."

Turning away from the window, Evie sat at the dressing table. "After Edgar served the refreshments, what else happened?"

While Phillipa tried to recall the details, Evie tapped her pen and wondered what else Batty might be willing to do for money…

The next morning

"What did I miss?" Evie asked as she took her place at the breakfast table.

Tom set his cup of coffee down. "The detective has begun his interviews. He wishes to speak to us individually."

"Well, he has already spoken with me. You and I will not come under suspicion."

Tom slanted his gaze toward Evie. "We're the only witnesses to the accident. For all anyone knows, we might have been responsible."

"Nonsense. Isabel will testify to the fact we were on the road and risked life and limb to get her out of the vehicle."

"What if she never recovers her senses?" Tom asked. "She looked in bad shape."

"What are you suggesting?"

"That it might be our word against… well, against anyone who decides to cast aspersions on our characters."

Evie snorted. "Who would do such a thing?"

"The killer, of course," Tom whispered. "It would be the perfect way to throw the scent off himself."

"Anyone who hears you would be right to accuse you of indulging in wild speculations. I hope Phillipa doesn't rely on suppositions for her mystery books. Remind me to tell her she will need clues and plenty of them, otherwise readers might complain."

A footman approached with a pot of coffee and poured some into Evie's cup.

"Whatever you do during your interview," Evie said,

"try to get the detective to tell you how Lorenzo died. He must know by now."

"How could he know? It takes time to perform an autopsy. The detective spent the night here. As far as I know, he didn't receive any telephone calls. And now he is in the library carrying out his interviews."

Evie gave it some thought. "We don't know if he came to Warwick Hall straight from the train station. He might have gone to the hospital first."

The door to the breakfast room opened and Charlie strode in. "The detective would like to speak with Unique now."

Unique remained seated, her eyes slightly glazed over.

"Unique."

She turned as if hearing Charlie for the first time. "I'm sorry, did you say something?"

Smiling, Charlie strode over to Unique, helped her up to her feet and, holding her hand, led her out of the breakfast room saying, "She's not a morning person."

"Someone must have had a late night," Evie murmured. When Charlie returned and took his place at the table, Evie found herself studying him. Moments later, she clicked her fingers.

"Are you using some sort of code?" Tom asked as he buttered some toast.

"No, I just remembered something Charlie said. You were there when he told us Lorenzo had..." Evie clicked her fingers again and tried to remember Charlie's exact words.

"Placed at the Indie 500?" Tom asked.

"Yes, that's it. He also said he knew some racing car

drivers who would be pleased to learn Lorenzo wouldn't be racing in this year's Indianapolis 500."

"And your point?"

"What if someone wanted to make sure he didn't race?"

Chapter Twelve

*E*vie considered getting another coffee but Tom had only now been called in to speak with Detective Inspector O'Neill and she knew he wouldn't be long. His succinct manner would ensure that. As everyone else had already been questioned by the detective, she expected to be next.

Smiling, she thought the detective had left the best until last. She gazed out the window and caught the last streaks of a bright orange sky.

Phillipa strode into the breakfast room. "Are you still here?"

"Yes, I'm waiting to be called in. Where is everyone else?"

Phillipa helped herself to a cup of coffee. "They're strolling around outside and making plans for the next leg of the trip. Will you be joining us?"

Evie decided she'd already had as much excitement as she could take. "I'm afraid I won't be able to. Someone has to take care of Isabel. She'll have to return to Halton House with us."

"How are you going to manage that? You're traveling in the roadster. I doubt she'll feel like sitting in the rumble seat. Not after the traumatic experience she went through."

"True. I hadn't given it any thought. I suppose I could telephone the house and ask Edmonds to drive up with the large car."

"Or," Phillipa said, "I could remain with you and I could drive Isabel back to your place."

Evie tilted her head. "Any chance you might then meander along a side road and end up in the north of England?" She held up a hand. "Give me a moment to savor the image and then I'll apologize for the callous remark." Despite her poor opinion of Isabel, Evie now felt responsible for her wellbeing.

She glanced at the door.

Tom had been gone longer than expected.

"What could they be talking about?"

"Perhaps Tom is sharing some of your insights with the detective," Phillipa suggested.

"What sort of questions did he ask you?"

Phillipa shrugged. "Nothing that surprised me. He wanted to know how well I knew everyone in the car rally group. He also wanted to know what everyone talked about when Isabel and Lorenzo arrived at Halton House."

"Did you tell him about the conversation we had last night?"

"No, I thought I'd leave that to you." Phillipa grinned. "I know just how much you enjoy chatting with the detective."

Evie glanced at the door again. "Did he actually say you were all free to go?"

Phillipa opened her mouth only to close it. Frowning, she finally said, "I honestly can't say if he did or didn't. Having said that, I can't think why he would force us to stay on."

Evie cupped her hands under her chin. "Did I tell you how Tom and I happened to be in the wrong place at the right time or vice versa?" When Phillipa shook her head, Evie continued, "We had a flat tire."

"I've had several of those," Phillipa said. "The last one actually sounded like a gunshot. I had a kneejerk reaction and threw my hands up in the air only to realize I needed to maintain control of the steering wheel. How did you get your flat tire?"

"That's just it. We don't know exactly how it happened. Tom suspects someone punctured it with a nail. Do you know anyone in the group capable of pulling such a stunt?"

Phillipa's cheeks turned a deep crimson.

Evie shifted to the edge of her chair. "You do."

"I couldn't say with absolute certainty." Phillipa brushed her hands across her face. "One of them pulled a prank and changed all my tires so I ended up with different sizes. I had a wobbly ride for several miles until they took pity on me and stopped to change them back. That was before I had learned to change my own tires."

Smiling, Evie said, "I'm going to take a wild guess and point the finger of suspicion at Charlie."

Phillipa lowered her eyes. "He's a grown-up kid."

"Is he likely to have tampered with Isabel's car?"

Giving a brisk shake of her head, Phillipa nibbled the tip of her thumb. "He couldn't have. He didn't have the opportunity to. When Isabel and Lorenzo finished their tea, they left and all the time they were in the drawing room, Charlie stood right there with them."

Tom entered the breakfast room and poured himself a cup of coffee.

When he didn't say anything, Evie asked, "Well? Did you get any information out of the detective?"

"No. Detective O'Neill is being guarded so I couldn't get anything out of him."

Evie surged to her feet and straightened her skirt. "Fine. I will give it my best shot."

"Oh... He didn't ask to see you."

"Pardon?"

Tom shrugged. "He said he already spoke with you."

Evie dug inside her pocket and retrieved the notes she had made the night before. "But I wanted to share this with him."

A footman entered. "Begging your pardon, milady. I thought you had finished."

"I suppose we should let you get on with your job."

The footman stood aside and said, "I believe the other guests are making their way to the drawing room for refreshments."

Phillipa wove her arm through Evie's. "Come on. We'll get to the bottom of this by subjecting them to such a fierce interrogation, they won't know what's hit them."

Evie gave a distracted nod but when they reached the drawing room, she stepped back and, excusing herself, strode off in the direction of the library, saying under her breath, "I can't believe he doesn't wish to speak with me."

She didn't bother knocking. Entering the book lined room, she sent her gaze skating around until she spotted the detective standing by the window, his hands clasped behind his back.

"Detective."

The detective turned, his eyebrows slightly raised as if she'd caught him by surprise.

"Lady Woodridge."

Evie's chin lifted. "How do you hope to carry out your investigation if you don't question everyone involved?"

"I'm sorry. I was under the impression I had spoken with everyone."

Evie slammed her hands against her waist. "Everyone except me. I thought you were keen to engage my assistance." Frowning, she crossed her arms. "Or are you? Now I think you were merely humoring me." She took a step toward him only to stop. The rumbling in her mind quietened and she experienced a moment of clarity.

Everything the detective had said to her the night before suddenly made sense. Or rather, as she viewed it all from a different perspective, the conversation acquired a different meaning.

Evie ran through the sequence of events. After the accident, Tom had gone to get help. A while later, he had returned saying the police wished them to remain because they needed to get witness statements. After which they'd been free to go to the Pecking Goose where the police had caught up with them again and had informed them a detective from Scotland Yard would be arriving soon...

"Wait a minute."

Startled, the detective's eyes widened.

"You lied to me," Evie accused.

"Pardon?"

"You led me to believe Isabel's family had been responsible for your involvement, but that can't be."

The detective clammed up.

"Admit it. They had nothing to do with it. They couldn't have. News about Isabel's accident could not have reached them so quickly. Not even if the constable had contacted the Embassy as soon as he identified the victims. Or sent a telegram directly to Isabel's family himself. That would be impossible because he would not have known how to contact Isabel's family in America."

The detective lifted his chin. "Her family has been contacted."

"When?"

"I don't recall exactly…"

"Before or after Scotland Yard became involved?" Evie demanded.

"I really don't see what this has to do with you not being questioned."

Evie held his gaze in a self-conceited attempt to coerce him into revealing more. If she were not so intent on getting results, she would laugh at herself.

The detective shook his head and pushed out a hard breath. "Lorenzo Bianchi has been a person of interest for quite some time."

Meaning Scotland Yard had already been involved. "Was it so hard to share that with me?"

"No, but I cannot stress this enough. It is highly inappropriate for me to share information with a member of the public. What is it about you, Lady Woodridge?" He looked around as if making sure no one would hear him. Lowering his voice, he said, "You have a way of extricating information out of me…"

Either that or the detective had been cunning in sharing something of little value in exchange for some future insight from Evie. She could never underestimate someone who made a living out of solving mysteries and served a higher purpose, seeking justice for those without voices.

Evie smiled. "Yes, I suppose I do." And just as well.

What could Lorenzo Bianchi have been involved in to warrant attention from Scotland Yard?

Chapter Thirteen

RED SKY IN THE MORNING, SHEPHERD'S WARNING

Tom's eyes danced around Evie's face, conveying a mixture of incredulity and amusement. "You spoke with the detective for two minutes and managed to get all that information out of him?"

Evie grinned. "I'm beginning to think I'm quite dazzling."

Tom studied her for a long moment. At one point, he brushed his hand across his chin, almost in frustration. "Exactly how did you manage it?" He tilted his head in thought. "I get the feeling I've said that before."

Hell hath no fury like a woman scorned, Evie thought. She knew she had walked into the library feeling somewhat slighted by the detective and had been determined to get answers from him.

"You must have worn him out," Tom said.

"In your own words, it only took me two minutes. That is certainly not enough time to wear anyone out." Evie lifted her chin in defiance. "I almost resent the implication."

"And you are well within your rights to do so. My apologies. I'm sure you employed subtle tact and asked the correct questions."

Evie cast an appreciative glance at the manicured lawn in front of them. Sir Richard might have been in mourning for a year, but his estate spoke of cheerful anticipation of the season. Flower beds bloomed with spring offerings. A couple of large earthenware urns flanked the entrance to Warwick Hall, the splashes of spring color contrasting the dark carved stonework of the pillars.

"As a matter of fact, I believe I did ask the right questions. However, my triumph is limited to extricating that one tidbit about Lorenzo Bianchi. The detective simply refused to add anything more. Now I have no option but to think the worst of Lorenzo Bianchi and we all know we shouldn't speak ill of the dead, so that puts me in an awkward position."

Tom laughed.

"I'm glad I can still be a source of amusement."

"Milady."

Evie turned.

A footman approached carrying a bouquet of flowers. "I hope these are satisfactory."

"Yes, thank you. They're beautiful blooms." Taking the bouquet, she said to Tom, "For Isabel. I thought she might need some cheering up. And now, I'm ready when you are. Or, at least, I will be after I've fetched my hat. Hold these for me, please." Handing the flowers to Tom, she rushed back inside Warwick Hall.

Along the way, she saw Marjorie and Unique studying a painting that covered the entire wall over the massive fireplace in the entrance hall. Two others emerged from the drawing room and joined them. Looking up, she saw Charlie and Batty coming down the stairs.

Evie had the strange feeling entering the house had set something into motion. Almost as if everyone had been waiting for her appearance to take up their positions and begin some sort of role playing.

"Lady Woodridge. Sir Richard has invited us to stay on for luncheon," Batty said. "Will you be joining us?"

"I dare say I will." She had no idea how long Isabel would be kept in hospital.

"We'll be setting off after that. Will you continue on with the car rally?"

Evie explained she would have to abandon the group. "Duty calls."

"In that case, it will be a farewell luncheon."

Along the rest of the way up the stairs, she encountered more of the car rally group, each person appearing to be doing nothing out of the ordinary and yet, in Evie's mind, they all looked suspicious.

In her room, she found the hat she wanted and spent a few minutes adjusting it on her head. A quick glance at her ensemble reminded her how well Caro matched her clothes. She had a great eye for detail.

If her maid could mingle with the car rally group, Evie had no doubt she would, in no time, find the culprit who had tampered with their tire.

Remembering she needed to telephone Halton House to organize Edmonds into driving down, she wondered if she should suggest he bring Caro along…

"She's sleeping at the moment. As for how she has been faring, I'm afraid she is in deep denial," the doctor said. "That's to be expected."

Evie handed the flowers to a nurse. "Does she sound lucid? Even if she doesn't accept what has happened, does she actually know where she is?"

"Yes, the nurse had a conversation with her about appropriate clothing for nursing staff. Mrs. Bianchi has a preference for what she called candy stripes, which she thinks would be far more cheerful than plain white. She talked at great length about the appropriate shade of red… or pink. I can't remember which."

The fact Isabel had managed to express an opinion set Evie's mind at ease. She had no doubt she would recover.

"Her family has been informed," the doctor continued. "I believe they are making their way from America and will arrive in five days."

This time, Evie nearly swooned with relief. The load that had been weighing on her like a ton of bricks lifted. Isabel would be better off surrounded by those who loved her, and they would most likely insist she return home to America.

The doctor cleared his throat. "She should be perfectly fine to leave hospital tomorrow."

"So early?"

The doctor nodded. "There is nothing physically wrong with Mrs. Bianchi. She will need a lot of attention and gentle caring. It is not unusual for those grieving to delay accepting the reality of the matter. I understand you are very good friends. Mrs. Bianchi spoke fondly of you."

"She did?" Evie couldn't help expressing her surprise.

The nurse murmured something in the doctor's ear. Turning to Evie, he excused himself saying, "I must attend to another patient. I trust we'll be seeing you again tomorrow." He looked down at Isabel. "If you wish, you may visit."

"Yes. Of course." Evie drew up a chair and sat next to the bed. Asleep, Isabel looked like an angel. Peaceful and content. She hoped her mind had chosen to go to a happy place.

"Hello, Isabel," she whispered. "I know you're sleeping…" Evie gave her hand a light pat. "I do hope you recover soon. It's… It's not easy at first." Looking over her shoulder to make sure no one would hear her, she added, "It's actually the pits. But as the saying goes, what doesn't kill you makes you stronger. It's what my mother said to me when I lost Nicholas and I know your mama. As I'm sure you already know, she would impart the same advice." She tried to think of other appropriate platitudes and then decided against saying more in case Isabel objected.

To Evie's surprise, Isabel stirred. Her eyes fluttered open and sighing, she made a dramatic gesture with her hand before letting it flutter back down as light as a feather wafting in the air.

When her lips moved, Evie leaned down. "That's all right, dear. You'll have plenty of time to speak when you are fully recovered." And she would, no doubt, try to make up for lost time, Evie thought.

When Isabel persevered, Evie offered her some water.

Isabel took a sip and then gestured for Evie to lean closer.

"Is there something else you need?" Evie asked. Leaning down, she tried to make out the whispered words but she had trouble understanding the slurred speech. When Evie moved to straighten, Isabel grabbed her hand and pulled her down again with surprising strength and determination.

"They killed him."

~

"And that's all she said?" Tom asked when Evie joined him outside.

Evie nodded. "I think the effort exhausted her. According to the doctor, the detective visited her an hour ago and tried to speak with Isabel but she didn't wake up. So, once again, I have done better than the esteemed detective. That's not to say I'm competing with him." Evie checked her watch. "Oh, heavens. We've missed lunch. Worse. The others will have left by now. I didn't even say goodbye to Phillipa."

Tom held the motor car door open for her. "We should get back. Those clouds look threatening."

Evie looked up. "Where did they come from? We had such beautiful, clear skies on the way here."

"They probably have something to do with the shepherd's warning sky we had this morning."

"Oh, yes. I remember seeing the bright orange streaks across the sky but I didn't connect it to the weather." Evie managed a light laugh. "For a moment there, I thought you were going to tell me about your joints being as good a warning as anything else."

Tom laughed. "There's nothing wrong with my joints yet. But I do have a great uncle who swears by the accuracy of their weather predictions. If he says it's going to rain, it does. No one ever dares to question great uncle Zachary."

"Did you just share personal information with me?"

He thought about it for a moment. "I believe I did."

"So, your great uncle Zachary really exists."

"Is there a reason why he wouldn't exist?"

"Where you're concerned, it's difficult to tell fact from fiction," Evie murmured just as the motor car roared to life.

"Pardon? I missed that."

"Never mind. Drive on, please. I don't wish to get wet."

"After what Isabel told you, I'd say that would be the least of your concerns."

Chapter Fourteen

RAINING PITCHFORKS AND DARNING NEEDLES (1866)

*S*everal miles before they reached Warwick Hall, the heavens opened up. Evie pulled up her collar, hunched her shoulders and hugged herself.

As the rain beat down, the wind picked up and stirred it, sending raindrops slashing in all directions.

With the visibility worsening, Tom had to slow down and by the time they drove through the gates leading to the Hall, they were both thoroughly drenched.

When the motor car stopped, Evie didn't wait for Tom to open the passenger door. Lunging out of the car, she ran as fast as she could, her feet sinking into the pebbled sludge. Keeping her head lowered, Evie tried to steer herself in the right direction. Then Tom reached out for her and pulled her along.

The front door opened and they burst inside, breaths gasping, their clothes dripping.

"I'm ever so sorry, Wilson."

The butler must have seen them coming. He stood at attention holding out a couple of large fluffy towels.

As Evie tried to dry herself off, she said, "We'll try to minimize the inconvenience and do all the dripping here."

She turned just as Wilson closed the door. In that brief instant, the curtain of rain eased and she thought she saw a vehicle.

"Oh… Is that another motor car? It looks familiar."

"It ought to," Tom said. "It's yours."

"Pardon?"

"It's the Duesenberg."

"Impossible. What is it doing here?"

"Begging your pardon, my lady." Wilson bowed his head slightly. "What with all the excitement, it slipped my mind. Your chauffeur arrived a short while ago."

"Really?" She hadn't had the opportunity to telephone Halton House to request that he drive down. What could have prompted him to drive here?

"Oh, milady. You're soaked through."

Hearing the familiar voice, Evie swung around. "Caro? What on earth are you doing here?"

"Well, someone had to come to your rescue." Caro hurried toward her, a couple of towels in her hands. "You're drenched. You need to change out of these clothes or you'll catch your death."

"Heavens. You'll need to fill in the gaps. We were only gone for an hour." Setting a foot on the stair, she stopped. "Oh, I hope Phillipa managed to avoid being caught in this deluge. It would be dreadfully dangerous to drive in these conditions."

"Don't worry about Phillipa," Caro cupped her elbow and drew her along. "She's nice and cozy in the library."

"She's still here?"

"They never left. Apparently, their luncheon dragged on and by the time they finished, it had already started to rain. Sir Warwick urged them all to stay another day."

By the time they reached her room, Evie's teeth were chattering.

"I'm going to draw you a hot bath, milady."

Sighing with relief, Evie sank into a tub full of deliciously steaming water. As Caro organized a crackling fire, she told her about the dowagers continuing raids of the attics.

"The footmen have been sworn to secrecy. The dowagers chose their moment well, coming in on the housekeeper's half day off. I didn't feel right asking what they were doing."

"Did you see what they took?"

Caro shook her head. "I'd been busy downstairs. If I hadn't gone up to put away some clothes, I would not have seen them at all. As it is, I only saw the horse drawn cart pulling away. I think there might have been a large trunk. Who knows what they stowed in there…"

Evie closed her eyes only to open them again. "You said you came to rescue me."

"Oh, yes…" Caro focused on poking the logs.

"Caro?"

"Oh… Well, news about the accident reached us when Sir Warwick contacted Lady Sara."

How much had Sir Richard told them? "Did the dowagers send you?"

"Not exactly."

"Well then… Who sent you?"

"No one. I mean, everyone downstairs talked a great deal about you driving off and the dangers of that road. It seems everyone had a story to tell about someone or other coming to some sort of misfortune. Then Edmonds told me about hearing noises during the night in the stable yard where the cars are kept…"

"Which night?"

"Before you left, milady."

Could Edmonds have heard the person responsible for tampering with their tire?

"Did he investigate?"

Caro nodded. "He said he hesitated because he knew strange things happen when there are large numbers of people staying at the house."

"What sort of strange things?"

"The occasional midnight rendezvous, drinking too much and wandering outside…"

That still didn't explain why Caro had felt compelled to come to her rescue.

Caro dipped her chin down and whispered, "I'd hate for something to happen to you."

"Dear Caro. Nothing will happen to me."

"I'm sorry I took the liberty…"

"Caro. Never apologize for being a caring person. I only wish you wouldn't worry so much. Remember, I have Tom with me."

Caro snorted. "Even with him around you ended up right in thick of it."

"He's hardly to blame for that," Evie said in her breeziest tone.

As she dressed, it occurred to ask, "Did you happen to notice anything else?"

"Such as what, milady?"

"Did you see Isabel when she arrived?"

"Oh, yes. My goodness. She made me think of those gusts of wind that swirl around in winter. She swept in and I could hear her from the upstairs hallway."

"Yes, her voice does tend to carry… and travel far. I suspect she might have had operatic training."

Caro gave her an impish smile. "When I noticed her arrival… I made a point of hovering."

Evie smiled and pictured Caro tiptoeing her way around the house, catching glimpses and hearing murmured conversations. "Oh, yes. Do tell."

"Don't get me wrong, milady. I don't make a habit of eavesdropping. The circumstances were such that I felt a strong obligation to keep an eye on things."

"I don't blame you, Caro. In your place, I would have done exactly the same. And I'm not just saying that to gain your confidence and encourage you to tell me all." Had she heard something useful?

Caro held up a dress for Evie to slip into. "I brought some decorative pieces, not the real valuable ones." She held up a small silver brooch with a kitten sitting up, its tail curled into an elegant curve.

"That's very thoughtful. Are you, by any chance, trying to avoid telling me what you heard?"

"It's done."

"Pardon?"

"That's what I heard, only… I can't tell you who said it. The voice sounded masculine but I couldn't tell you with any certainty if it came from a man. Earlier, I happened to hear one of the women delivering a few lines in a male voice. I think she might be an actress. So,

I might have heard someone mimicking a man… Anyhow, I had been making my way along the gallery when I heard the murmured remark. I tried to look down to see but they moved away into the drawing room."

"Would you be able to recognize the voice if you heard it again?"

"I'm sure I would."

It's done.

What on earth could that mean? "Did you hear it before or after Isabel and Lorenzo left?"

"After and that's not all I heard." Caro scooped in a breath. "During their last raid…"

Evie's eyebrows hitched up slightly. Raid? "Whose?"

"The dowagers' raid. They had an argument. Lady Henrietta said she couldn't help being an Edwardian through and through and adhering to the practices of the day." Tilting her head, Caro asked, "What do you think that means?"

"I'd actually be both afraid and intrigued to ask the dowager for an explanation. It all depends on the point she is trying to put across. On one occasion, I remember her saying she favored the Victorian era over the Edwardian only to change her mind the following day saying she had lived in the cusp of both eras so she felt entitled to feel either way."

Caro rubbed her temple.

Smiling, Evie said, "Yes, sometimes, her reasoning makes my head throb too." Seeing Caro still looking rather perplexed, Evie put her mind to work. "Let's see. The Victorians were incredibly conservative. While the Edwardians had a less rigid standard of conduct. Just look at the way we dressed."

"So, which era are we in now?"

"Some people would say we are in the midst of the Georgian era because of King George, but I'm inclined to think of this as the Jazz era. So… what could have prompted Henrietta to remark upon her behavior? She must have been justifying something." Evie clicked her fingers. "Oh, maybe her pilfering. I shouldn't really call it that since I feel she still owns everything in Halton House."

"She might have been talking about your relationship with Tom Winchester," Caro suggested.

"Are you referring to our working relationship?"

Caro's cheeks filled with a tinge of pink. "Or she might have been referring to the car rally group." Caro gave a firm nod. "Yes, that must be it. Their behavior is hardly exemplary. They hoot and cheer for no reason at all and the way they dress… Lady Henrietta must have thought the house had been taken over by a carnival."

"If you can think of anything else you might have seen or heard, don't hesitate to tell me, Caro."

"Why? Has something happened?" Caro gasped. "Of course, it has. Your friend's husband died in a car accident." Caro gasped again. "I meant to ask. Why is the detective here?"

"He's still here?"

"Yes. Apparently, he had left to call in on the village and then he returned soon after Edmonds and I drove up. The staff here have been rather tightlipped about his presence."

He must have gone directly from his failed visit with Isabel back to Warwick House…

Evie wondered how much she should share with Caro without sending her scurrying for cover. Her maid would hate the idea of being in a house with a possible murderer. And, after Isabel's whispered revelation, and the remark Caro had heard…

Evie had to assume the worst.

Chapter Fifteen

"Detective. I see you are still with us. I thought you had given everyone leave to go on their merry way."

"Not exactly, Lady Woodridge."

Evie stilled. "I must have been misinformed." Earlier that day, Phillipa had said everyone had been questioned and… they were all ready to leave. Then Batty and Charlie had told her they would be leaving after luncheon.

"Can you tell me where you were headed before the accident?" he asked.

"Portsmouth. At least, that had been the intended destination. I thought I'd already told you that."

He nodded. Drawing out his notebook, he flipped through the pages. "And Miss Brady had been traveling up north."

"Yes, she got lost."

"Do you know where Miss Brady is now?"

"I assumed she would be here." Evie looked around the library and saw Tom approaching. He had changed his suit and looked clean-shaven. "Tom, have you seen Phillipa?" Even as she asked, a feeling of trepidation swept through her. Shaking her head, she dismissed it. What could possibly happen to any of them while they stayed at Warwick Hall?

"She's probably in one of the drawing rooms. I'll go look for her."

"That's all right, Mr. Winchester. I'll be happy to speak with her whenever it's convenient. We're not going anywhere for some time. This storm is not easing up."

Evie considered bartering with the detective but thought better of it. He needed to know what Isabel had told her.

Lorenzo Bianchi had died for a reason. "Detective. I visited Isabel in hospital…" She told the detective what Isabel had revealed.

"You don't look surprised, detective." Evie drummed her fingers on the armrest. "I feel I am well within my rights to be informed. It looks as if we will all be spending the night at Warwick Hall and I would like to know if we are in any danger."

He held up his hand. "Rest assured, these people don't wish to draw attention to themselves."

"These people?"

"I don't wish to alarm you, Lady Woodridge."

"I am already alarmed but only because I feel I am being kept in the dark."

Hitching his hands on his hips, the detective swung away. A moment later, he turned to face her again. Evie found it all very dramatic.

"This incident involves organized crime."

Evie's eyebrows shot up. "We're in the English countryside. I expect to find that sort of activity taking place in… in the seedier side of London or the wharves."

"I'm glad to see you are not completely ignorant of such goings on."

"Detective, I would be the first to admit to leading an insulated life but that doesn't make me ignorant of the facts of life."

The detective looked down at the floor and, after a brief deliberation, he said, "We believe Lorenzo Bianchi had been involved in trafficking."

Evie entertained all sorts of possibilities. Back home, prohibition had been in full swing for several months and already there had been reports of illegal activities. But no such embargo existed in England so it couldn't be liquor.

Evie drew in a deep breath and looked the detective in the eye. "I realize you may not be at liberty to say, but I would be greatly interested to learn how Lorenzo Bianchi died."

"His heart ceased."

Evie sat back and crossed her arms. "That's an interesting way of saying he had a heart attack."

The detective mirrored her crossed arms.

Evie imagined anyone walking into the room would think they were about to lock horns.

"What could have caused the attack?" she wondered out loud. "I only met him the one time and he looked quite healthy. Regardless, he might have suffered from some sort of heart condition. Yes? No?"

The detective didn't even bat an eyelash so Evie decided to talk until he gave something away. "I know he stopped briefly at Halton House and had a cup of tea. Then he rushed to catch up with me. So that would not have given him time to stop and indulge in a large meal that might have triggered some sort of attack. As a car racing driver, he would have been used to driving at great speeds, so we have to cross that out too."

Evie held up a finger and entertained an idea she couldn't share with the detective. Smiling to herself, she pictured Isabel talking her husband to death. After a moment, she found the thought in bad taste and so dismissed it.

Evie looked away, gasped and clasped her hand against her mouth, prompting the detective to uncross his arms.

"Lady Woodridge. Are you all right?"

The detective had mentioned Lorenzo had been involved in trafficking. Over the last few years, she had read articles about the growing cocaine problem and its effects on society…

Evie nodded and, leaning forward slightly, she whispered, "Drugs?"

As the word hung between them, Phillipa entered the library. "Here you are. What have I missed?"

Lifting the cup of coffee to his lips, Tom murmured, "You're still fuming."

Evie glared at the detective. When Phillipa had made an appearance, he had taken her aside to have a word with her. Despite remaining in the library, he had chosen the opposite corner, putting enough distance between himself and Evie.

"He is being so obviously secretive. I don't understand why he bothers. He must know Phillipa will share everything with us. And, yes. I am still fuming. He only needed to nod. Would it have killed him to give a miniscule sign as confirmation Lorenzo Bianchi had been involved in cocaine trafficking?"

Tom laughed.

Huffing, Evie said, "As for you laughing, you could at least pretend to be supportive. I'm sure you are just as curious as I am."

Evie poured herself another cup of tea and sat back to watch the rain. The wind had eased down but the rain continued, making it inadvisable for the car rally group to set out.

Taking an impatient sip of her tea, she asked, "Do you think there is a connection between Lorenzo and someone from the car rally group?" When Tom didn't answer, she nudged him with the tip of her shoe. "Am I boring you?"

"Never. I'm deep in thought trying to play your game of connect the dots. We now know his heart ceased."

Evie nodded. "Since the detective refuses to share any other information, it is up to us to discover what can make a heart cease."

"Drugs," Tom suggested.

"Is that so? I'm afraid I don't know much about the detriments of drug usage. Well… other than what I have read in the newspapers and that information can't always be trusted. Sometimes I feel they are trying to manipulate the way I think. If I am going to be misinformed, I would prefer to remain ignorant." She finished her tea and set the cup down.

A footman appeared and cleared the small table. "Will there be anything else, milady?"

"No, thank you." Glancing at Tom who had now picked up a magazine, she asked, "What has you so intrigued?"

"You." He turned the magazine so Evie could see for herself.

"What am I looking at? Oh… Oh… That's me. Being hugged by Lorenzo Bianchi at the Automobile Club."

Pointing at another photograph, Tom said, "And here you are again, having dinner with your best friend."

"Sir Richard said he kept numerous newspapers. Where did you get that from?"

"I found this in a drawer." Tom pointed at the book-case behind him. It had several shelves with large drawers on the bottom part.

Opening one, Evie saw the newspapers had been folded and stacked, slightly overlapping and allowing for easy access to the date on the top. "I suppose there is a system here."

Tom handed her what looked like a small ruler. "I believe this is used as a placeholder to mark the spot where you remove something. There are a number of them in that little box on the bottom shelf."

"In other words, don't mess with the system." Evie looked inside another drawer and found a stack of ladies' magazines. "He certainly doesn't discriminate." Then again, these might have been part of his wife's subscription. Evie had never bothered to cancel Nicholas' subscriptions. The newspapers and journals on agriculture and business continued to arrive each month as if nothing had happened.

"Who are the other people in the photograph?" Tom asked.

Taking a chair beside Tom, Evie had a closer look. She pointed to two of the men. "They are racing car drivers and this other man is an engineer. I can't remember what his field of expertise is. I didn't realize it at the time, but Isabel and I were the only women at the table. It seems car racing is a male dominated world."

Tom quirked his eyebrow. "At least until a woman decides to take it up."

"Don't look at me. If I need to travel from point A to point B, I wish to be able to admire the scenery at leisure."

"Never say never," Tom murmured under his breath.

"Out of curiosity, would you teach me to drive?"

Tom set his magazine down and gazed up at the ceiling. "Yes."

"Without reservations?"

He shook his head. "Absolutely. What if something were to happen to your driver? You'd be stuck. It makes perfect sense for you to learn."

Tapping her foot, Evie mused, "I'd have to get a smaller car. Perhaps a roadster. I believe the idea is beginning to grow on me." She tilted her head in thought and then asked, "Were you being diplomatic when you agreed you would teach me to drive?"

Tom's eyes crinkled at the edges. "Did I actually agree to teach you? I think I might have expressed a hypothetical willingness to undertake the task."

Rolling her eyes at him, Evie took the magazine he'd been perusing from him and had a closer look at the photographs. "I must say, my public mask serves me well. You can hardly tell I'd been entertaining ways of ending it all."

Surprise registered in Tom's eyes. "That bad?"

Evie nodded. "I had to take a powder before bed. My head wouldn't stop pounding." She narrowed her gaze and lifted the journal for a closer inspection. "Did you notice this man in the background? He appears in both photographs and they were both taken at different times. One at luncheon and the other at dinner. And he's wearing the same suit."

Shaking his head, Tom said, "If Isabel Bianchi has such a negative effect on you, why didn't you try to make your getaway after lunch?"

"Isabel never left my side. Not even when I used the pretext of having to change for dinner." Evie tapped the photograph. "It can't be a coincidence. He's looking directly at Lorenzo."

Tom leaned in for a closer look. "Do you think he'd been keeping tabs on him? He could just be a racing enthusiast."

Evie glanced over at the detective. "Sir Richard pointed the finger of suspicion at Halton House. Maybe we need to look further back." Even so, something had happened. In her own house, she thought. "I'm so glad Henrietta and Sara are not here. I have the strangest feeling… before this night is over, we'll be talking a great deal about finances. They are English through and through and would not tolerate it." Evie tapped her chin.

"What else is on your mind?" Tom asked.

"Phillipa. When she walked into the pub, she looked somber. That's not like her. I know I've only met her recently, but she simply doesn't come across as the type to even frown."

The detective and Phillipa stood up and, after another brief exchange, they joined Evie and Tom.

"See. She's frowning," Evie murmured.

"Who's frowning?" Phillipa asked.

"You."

Phillipa and the detective pulled up a couple of chairs and sat down.

"I'm afraid I've landed in a bit of a pickle," Phillipa said.

"Does it have something to do with you getting lost?" Evie asked and thought one could be excused for taking a wrong turn, but to actually end up in the wrong part of the country would require a great deal of disorientation.

"Getting lost?" Phillipa shook her head. "I went precisely where I'd been told to go."

The detective nodded. "And the places Phillipa visited happen to be marked as places of interest for trafficking."

A footman approached. "There is a telephone call for Detective Inspector O'Neill."

As the detective left to answer the call, Evie murmured, "I am so tempted to say we outnumber him and could force him to share the news, but I suppose we shall have to rely on his goodwill."

"Pity," Phillipa said. "I would have given anything to see you trying to wrench the information out of him."

Exchanging a look with Tom, Evie said, "There is one other person we outnumber." She looked at Phillipa. "Kindly fill in the gaps and tell us what you were talking about with the detective."

Chapter Sixteen

"A HAPPY-GO-LUCKY; NEITHER CRAVEN NOR VALIANT."
MOBY DICK (1851)

*E*vie crossed her legs and swung her foot from side to side. Half an hour after hearing Phillipa's tale, she still struggled to understand why Phillipa had blindly followed instructions left by an unknown person.

Tom handed Evie a cup of tea. "It's chamomile."

"Are you suggesting I need to calm down?"

"At the risk of incurring your wrath, I'd just like to say fretting won't help."

Evie's foot tapped the air. "You actually expect me to be perfectly at ease with the idea of Phillipa searching her trunk and finding several packages with instructions to deliver them to several locations in the north of England. Foolish girl. I don't understand what she could have been thinking." Evie sat up and stomped her foot on the floor. "She's lucky she's not behind bars." Grumbling under her breath, she added, "What if something had happened to her?" She looked up at Tom. "I know you're now going to be the voice of reason but I am allowed to indulge in a rant, which in turn makes me feel old. Are they so happy-go-lucky they give no thought to consequences?"

"I suppose you're referring to the bright young things."

Evie sat back and drank her tea. "I'm inclined to think there is nothing bright about them."

"You know I can hear you," Phillipa said.

"Yes, but is anything I am saying sinking in?" Evie asked.

Phillipa inspected her nails. "None of us made a big deal out of it."

The detective entered the library and appeared to hesitate. Evie didn't blame him. Her head throbbed from holding her scowl in place.

"You'll be pleased to hear I have no intention of beating about the bush," he said. "Lorenzo Bianchi's death is now being attributed to an overdose. Specifically, cocaine."

Evie glanced at Phillipa. Before she could say anything, Phillipa jumped to her own defense. "I didn't know I had been trafficking that substance. As far as I knew, the parcels contained nothing more than dressmaking material. In fact, the addresses I delivered the items to were dressmaking establishments."

The detective cleared his throat. "The coroner had some other interesting findings."

"We're listening." Evie could barely hide her surprise at his willingness to share more information.

"He found another substance in the victim's system. Barbituric acid."

"That sounds rather ghastly," Evie remarked.

"And yet, you are probably quite familiar with a

particular product named Veronal. It is used to cure insomnia."

Evie slid to the edge of her seat. "Are you suggesting he fell asleep at the wheel?"

"Quite possibly. We believe Veronal had been mixed with cocaine. The coroner described the symptoms as sluggishness, incoordination, difficulty in thinking and shallow breathing. High dosages have been recently recorded as being responsible for victims falling into a coma and eventual death."

"And this substance is being trafficked?" Evie asked.

The detective shook his head. "We have only come across cocaine. This leads us to believe Lorenzo Bianchi had been deliberately given or sold a deadly mix."

Evie slumped back on her chair only to surge to her feet and stride to the window. Not that she could see much since the rain continued to pelt down.

"Why?" Evie asked.

"He might have annoyed the wrong people," the detective suggested.

Evie looked over her shoulder and said, "If you suspected him of trafficking, then you must have been on his trail."

The detective gave a reluctant nod. "We learned of his involvement in the trafficking business only a short while ago. We believe he transported the drugs into the country. By the time the information reached us, he had already disembarked."

"Did you search his vehicle, his trunks…?"

"Until now, we only had circumstantial evidence and no actual proof. Lorenzo Bianchi had been seen with dubious characters already suspected of dealing in cocaine."

Why would someone like Lorenzo Bianchi become involved in something so… wicked? Even if he didn't have any money, he had certainly married into it.

Evie swung around to face them. "Phillipa, you implied they all followed instructions without question. Does that mean the others are involved too? Please tell me you were not the only one duped into delivering drugs."

Phillipa's cheeks colored. "I'm afraid we have all performed deliveries at one time or another. It seemed like an easy way to earn some extra cash. I had no reason to question the contents of the packages. And, more often than not, the person receiving the package would say they'd been waiting so long for that particular cloth and how Mrs. so and so would be delighted because she would finally get her dress."

Looking at the detective, Evie asked, "Are you hoping Isabel will be able to fill in the gaps?"

He nodded. "The thought occurred to me."

Good luck with that, Evie thought, knowing he would get far more than he bargained for.

The detective added, "However, we're not sure how reliable her information will be. After all, she was married to him and she might choose to remain loyal to the bonds of marriage."

Tom waved the magazine they'd been perusing.

Oh, yes. The person of interest in the photographs.

When Tom showed him the photographs, a splash of red settled on the detective's cheeks. "He's one of ours. A police officer working undercover."

"And now gracing the pages of a ladies' magazine. Not much of a cover." Checking the time, Evie said,

"I'm going upstairs to change and to take a break from this mayhem."

Along the way, Evie wondered about those photographs. If the police had been keeping an eye on Lorenzo Bianchi, could there be someone else the police might identify as a person of interest?

She entered her room just as she began to entertain ideas about betrayals and deceptions. If Lorenzo had been working for traffickers, he would have dealt with people who probably wouldn't think twice about turning against one of their own or killing them.

She found Caro going through a suitcase.

Looking up, Caro asked, "Have you made any progress?"

Smiling, Evie sat down at the dressing table. "What makes you think I am in any way involved in the investigation?"

"I'd be surprised if you weren't. I'm sure the detective knows you have a greater chance of gaining information from Isabel, what with you being her best friend."

Evie turned to look at Caro. She had to wait a full minute before her maid chuckled.

"I'm ever so sorry, milady. I just can't stop thinking about your friend saying you had perished with the Titanic. How is she, by the way?"

"This might sound insensitive, but I believe she will recover in no time. In her youth, Isabel made a pledge to never go into deep mourning. In her opinion, life should always be about living in the moment and always moving on."

"She might have changed her attitude after she married," Caro suggested.

"I doubt it. For as long as I've known Isabel, she has always adhered to her own brand of raison d'être. She believes she leads her life with purpose."

"I'd be interested to know what she thinks you do."

"I'm withering away, of course. And that would be putting it mildly. She thinks I live in town. The moment she finds out I am now determined to make a life in Berkshire, she will have a field day. I wouldn't be surprised if she tries to intervene and rescue me from a life of wretched boredom."

Caro held up a dress. "I brought this pale pink dress for you to wear at dinner. You seem to be neglecting it."

"Yes, I'm not really sure about the shade. Next time I organize a new wardrobe, I want you right there with me, Caro. You have exquisite taste." Stepping back, Evie gave Caro a head to toe assessment. Evie smiled as an idea took shape in her mind. "We're just about the same height."

"I'm a little shorter but thank you for saying so. I've always wanted to be taller."

Taking the dress from Caro, Evie held it up against her.

"Milady?"

"Give me a minute."

"Please don't take this the wrong way, milady, but having been in your employ for some years now, I know a lot can happen in a minute."

"Yes, I think the dress would suit you better. Try it on." Seeing Caro hesitating, Evie urged, "Go on."

"Now?"

"Yes, now."

"But…"

"Just put the dress on."

Moments later, Caro stood in the middle of the room looking as stiff as a board.

"I think you forgot to breathe."

"Sorry, milady."

No, that wouldn't do at all, Evie thought. "It's Evie tonight."

"Sorry, Evie." Caro frowned. "Pardon?"

"Well, I have an idea." Evie stepped back again and tapped her chin as she worked out some of the details in her mind. "I'll tell you about it in a minute."

"During the last minute you requested, I ended up wearing your dress. I'm almost afraid to ask, but I must... What can you possibly have planned for the next minute?"

Evie circled around Caro and declared, "Perfect."

"I'm glad you think so."

"Now for the shoes." Evie opened a small trunk. "These ones will do nicely. Here, put them on."

"But..."

"And your hair." Taking Caro by the shoulders, she guided her to the stool in front of the dresser. "I thought you were going to try to make it more fashionable."

"It's hardly a pressing issue with me, milady. I don't have to look my best. I mean, not in the way you do."

"We could try a headband."

"Shouldn't you be getting ready for dinner?"

"Yes, in a minute. We need to sort you out first. Oh..." Swinging away, Evie pulled on the bell. A few minutes later, a footman appeared. "Could you please let Wilson know there will be an extra guest for dinner? I'll make my apologies for the intrusion to Sir Warwick myself."

"At once, milady."

When the footman left, Evie turned her focus back to Caro's transformation. "Tonight, my dear, you are going to be Miss…" Evie leaned forward. "Heavens, all this time I've insisted on calling you Caro. I've forgotten your family name."

"Thwaites, milady."

"Well, Caro Thwaites. You are my companion."

"I knew a lot could happen in a minute," Caro murmured. "May I ask why I am suddenly to become your companion?"

"I want you to mingle with the bright young things and find the culprit."

Caro gasped. "Culprit?"

"Someone in this house is guilty of something and I believe you can unmask them. I have always thought you had a keen eye for detail. It's time we put it to some really good use. As Lady Henrietta would say, tally-ho."

Chapter Seventeen

LADY CAROLINA THWAITES I PRESUME?

"I can't believe I'm doing this," Caro whispered.

"I'd suggest you follow my lead. However, I think you know how to get about. I trust your instinct."

Caro tugged Evie back. "Are we just going to walk into the drawing room?"

"Would you like to be announced?" Evie smiled. "I should have given you a title. In fact, it's not too late. You could be Lady Thwaites, my distant cousin twice removed. I've only just discovered I have an English cousin."

"And I appeared from out of nowhere?"

Evie nodded. "Yes, I will be letting everyone know you are very peculiar and they shouldn't mind your curious ways."

"But Sir Warwick has already seen me. He knows I'm your maid."

Evie shook her head. "He saw Caro, my maid. You are my cousin Caroline Thwaites."

"It's actually Carolina. My mother wanted me to be slightly different and stand out from the crowd."

"There you go. We are in agreement. You are different." Evie slid her arm through Caro's and strode in. "Everyone, I'd like you to meet my distant cousin, Lady Carolina Thwaites."

Sir Richard smiled and raised his glass. Tom gave her a lifted eyebrow look that spoke of questioning her sanity. Phillipa clapped her hands. While everyone else waited for individual introductions.

Evie smiled. "You are already a smashing success. See, I told you it would be easy."

"You said no such thing, you wicked child."

Evie gave Caro a worried look. "Did you just try to sound like the dowager? We are the same age, I'm sure."

"I'd like permission to be a few days older so I can take the opportunity to chastise you."

This time, Evie frowned. "Is this something you've wanted to do for some time?"

"It has been a fantasy of mine." Caro gave her a wide grin.

"You seem to be adapting to your new station in life with great gusto. Keep it up and remember, try to engage everyone in conversation." Looking up, Evie smiled at Sir Richard. "My cousin, Carolina."

"Delighted to meet you."

To her surprise, Sir Richard played along without a glitch.

"I hope our rain hasn't given you the wrong impression about our little part of the world. We take great pride in our spring sunshine."

"Tom, this is my cousin, Lady Carolina Thwaites."

Caro smiled. "Oh, please, call me Carolina."

Tom took Caro by her arm saying, "Let me introduce you around."

Congratulating herself on a marvelous idea, Evie turned to Sir Richard. "It's very sporting of you to join in the charade."

"Whatever do you mean?"

"Oh… Well. Never mind." Had he not noticed Caro and Carolina were one and the same person? "You must be delighted to see the end of the rain. We should all be able to get on our way tomorrow."

"Unless the detective says you must stay on," Sir Richard said.

"Is that likely to happen? He has spoken with everyone. If he'd found something odd, he would have taken someone into custody."

"Yes, you might be right. I'm afraid I'm in one of my moods and not likely to be good company tonight." Sir Richard sighed. "Lady Warwick would have been delighted by this gathering. She loved her soirees and house parties."

Evie thought Sir Richard must have married young. He didn't look a day over fifty.

"It's good to see young Hemsworth out and about enjoying himself." Sir Richard gave a slow shake of his head. "He'll have a job and a half trying to keep the estate together."

"You're familiar with it?"

He gave a small nod. "North of here in Buckinghamshire. In my youth, I attended a few shooting weekends at Hemsworth House. The place is crumbling around them. It's a pity and now possibly too late for them to recover. It's all about keeping up with the times and adjusting to new methods, something they haven't been able to do. One must never attach oneself to the familiar." He made a gesture with his hand. "Always remember to bend with the wind of change."

"So, what do you think Batty will do when he inherits his crumbling estate?"

"He'll either be imaginative or pragmatic and sell."

"What about the tenants?"

"Oh, they've long gone. Hence their downfall. The farms were the first to fall and without that income, they relied on what little money they could borrow. I believe there were also some bad investments."

Would Batty consider trafficking as a lucrative business to get into in order to keep his estate running? He seemed to make a habit of utilizing his strengths to get by. Evie had to admit hiring himself out as a batsman for struggling cricket teams had been a genius idea.

What if Batty had masterminded the delivery of packages by using the car rally group?

According to Phillipa, she had found the packages containing the cocaine in the trunk of her car. Someone in the group had to be responsible for putting the parcels there. She couldn't think of any other explanation.

"You're looking pensive, Lady Woodridge," Sir Richard said. "I hope you're not experiencing difficulties back home. I would be surprised if you were."

Pushing her thoughts aside, Evie smiled. "Oh, no. The estate is in fine hands. My husband made sure of that."

"Oh, yes. Nicholas Halton. I met him a couple of times. A forward-thinking man, always on the lookout for ways to improve his farming techniques and making sure his tenants flourished along with him." Sir Richard laughed. "I say, your cousin Carolina is quite a star."

Evie scanned the room and found Caro surrounded

by the bright young things who appeared to be hanging on her every word.

Tom strode toward her and engaged Sir Richard in conversation. That freed Evie to move around and target someone who might inadvertently reveal something of worth. Excusing herself, she made a beeline for Unique but before she could reach her, the detective strode into the room and intercepted Evie.

"My apologies for appearing underdressed, Lady Woodridge."

"I'll survive, I'm sure."

He took stock of all the people in the drawing room and asked, "Who is that lady holding so many guests enthralled?"

"Oh, that's my second cousin twice removed, Lady Carolina Thwaites."

"I didn't realize your cousin had traveled with you. You didn't mention her."

"An oversight. As you can see, she doesn't require any assistance with promoting herself." Caro's ability had Evie mesmerized. What could she be talking about?

The detective asked, "Did she come into contact with Lorenzo Bianchi?"

"You needn't worry about questioning Carolina. She is far too self-involved to notice anything or anyone."

"So, you are quite prepared to vouch for her."

"Of course. She is, after all, my cousin."

"Twice removed," the detective said and tapped his chin in thought. "She reminds me of someone."

"Oh, Carolina reminds many people of someone else. We often joke she could become a spy because she has this wonderful ability to mimic people and blend in.

You know, she aspired to be an actress, but her mama wouldn't hear of it."

"And still she reminds me of someone. That's often a worry with people in my profession. We come across so many criminals, everyone we meet begins to acquire the characteristics."

Grinning, Evie said, "I hope you don't make the same comparisons when you look at me." Trying to change the subject, she asked, "Did you discover anything new from the photographs Tom showed you?"

The detective shook his head. "The detective put in charge of following Lorenzo confirmed he only came into contact with the people appearing on the photograph."

"He might have found other ways to communicate with a co-conspirator."

"Such as?"

Evie thought about it for a moment. "If someone wishes to pass on a message to me, they don't necessarily have to do it in person. They could... leave a note in my room."

Evie remembered Caro saying Edmonds had heard noises in the night. Could that have been someone stowing the cocaine packages in the trunks? Perhaps Lorenzo employed the same tactic and had an arrangement with someone to simply deposit the package in his motor car... "I assume you have searched his wrecked vehicle."

The detective gave a knowing smile. "I wondered if you would get around to connecting the dots."

"Pardon?"

"Several packages were found in Lorenzo Bianchi's trunk."

"Were they parceled up in such a way as to camouflage them?"

He slipped his hands inside his pockets and studied her long and hard. "Have you ever considered becoming a detective?"

"Oh, heavens. No, however, there is some interest in me becoming a writer. Specifically, a mystery writer. You might want to look into it yourself. I'm sure you have come across many interesting murder cases."

"Yes and, lately, most of them somehow... involve you."

A footman approached them with a tray of drinks.

"Oh, these look divine," Evie exclaimed.

"Cocktails, my lady."

Evie helped herself to a glass. "Detective, I believe you still owe me an answer."

"And I am reluctant to provide it," he admitted.

"You didn't notice any similarities in the packages?"

"The constable located the cocaine and passed on the information during one of our telephone conversations. Remember, I have been stuck here for most of the day."

When he didn't continue, Evie said, "Did the constable also give you detailed information about the packages."

Setting his drink down, he drew out his notebook and made a note. "I wouldn't want to forget."

"With so much happening, I'm surprised you don't get around with a personal assistant to take notes." She held the glass to her lips only to lower it again. Evie told him about her chauffeur, Edmonds, hearing noises in the night. "Could this have been the trafficker depositing his packages?"

The detective looked around the drawing room, his expression concerned.

"Are you about to tell me you haven't searched anyone else's motor car?"

"If you recall, Lady Woodridge, it has been raining ceaselessly. The motor cars are not going anywhere."

"Yes, but if word spreads, they might all try to dispose of the packages."

"Phillipa Brady promised to keep the information to herself."

Evie harrumphed, mostly in jest. "I'm surprised you are prepared to trust Phillipa. Don't get me wrong. She is rather sweet but her loyalties might tip in favor of her friends. Then again, she is keen to get to the bottom of this and find Lorenzo's killer. I withdraw my suspicions." Looking at the detective, Evie asked, "If I had to guess I'd say you are having second thoughts about searching the vehicles."

His jaw muscles twitched, much the same way Tom's did when he tossed an idea around.

"If I go out now, it would mean disrupting the gathering and Sir Warwick has been far too accommodating for me to do that to him."

"Heavens," Evie exclaimed.

"You disapprove of my lax modus operandi?"

"Not at all. However, I just remembered something my maid overheard."

"What's that?"

"It's done." Evie explained how Caro hadn't been able to identify the person speaking but, in her opinion, it had sounded like a man's voice or a woman impersonating a man. "When I received a telegram advising me of Isabel's arrival the next day, I immediately asked my maid to pack my bags." Had someone overheard her? She had been in her room, but someone might have been standing outside her bedroom door trying to eavesdrop.

"Tom needs to check his roadster. I wouldn't want to be accused of trafficking and hauled away to prison."

Chapter Eighteen

THE JOY OF JOYS IS THE PERSON OF LIGHT BUT
UNMALICIOUS HUMOR - EMILY POST

*E*njoying her smoked salmon entrée, Evie tried to set aside her reservations.

Yes, she would have preferred prompt action, however, the detective had insisted on waiting until after dinner to carry out a search of the motor cars, saying he didn't wish to arouse anyone's suspicions.

She had to trust he knew best…

She turned to Lord Braithwaite, Charlie to his friends, who sat on her right. "How did you find Carolina?"

"Highly entertaining," he said. "She regaled us with tales about her maid."

"Did she, indeed…" Evie gave him her full attention.

"Hobson is fiercely protective of Carolina and has been known to wander around the grounds in the middle of the night to make sure no one tries to break into the house."

Hobson?

It took a moment for Evie to realize Caro had given

herself a maid. And, in her own way, she had issued a threat to anyone wishing to get up to no good during the night. They would do so at their own risk.

"I suppose that serves as a warning to stay indoors tonight lest Hobson mistakes someone for an intruder. I hear she is quite handy with a walking stick. I also hear said walking stick has a secret attachment."

"I think after this sumptuous meal, we shall all sleep like babies." Charlie gave her a pensive look. "If you ever decide to join another car rally, I suggest you limit your lunch to something light. We learned the hard way full meals tend to make people sleepy and therefore hopeless on the road."

Lorenzo and Isabel had traveled in the morning, so he couldn't possibly be referring to them.

She arranged some salmon on her fork and tried to stop herself from asking if Charlie had found any packages in his motor car. She couldn't risk interfering with the police investigation. When the urge to ask persevered, she forced herself to focus on her meal.

Trying to take her mind off the packages, Evie asked, "What sort of motor car do you drive?"

"It's a 1919 Meisenhelder."

"That doesn't sound British."

"It's American."

Evie turned to the young man seated on her other side, Anthony Wright, and asked what he drove.

"A Morris Cowley."

"Oh, yes. That one sounds British."

Charlie scoffed. "All the parts are made in America."

That triggered a discussing about the latest models and plans to acquire them.

They must have all been well rewarded for delivering

those packages. Otherwise, how could they afford to purchase such expensive vehicles?

With the meal coming to an end, Evie realized it would be up to her to lead the ladies into the drawing room and leave the gentlemen to their cigars and port.

This would be her opportunity to catch up with Caro and Phillipa who had both been sitting opposite her and had actively engaged their dinner table companions in conversation.

"Carolina, how did you enjoy your meal?" Evie asked as they made their way to the drawing room.

Looking around her, Caro lowered her voice and said, "Now that I've had a taste of how the upper crust dine, I might mount my own revolution and demand à la carte dining for the downstairs staff."

Caro's impish smile suggested she had made the remark in jest, but one never knew...

"But you already enjoy that. Mrs. Horace takes great pride in cooking for the staff."

"Oh... yes, I suppose she does."

At the risk of inciting a full-blown revolution, Evie asked, "Is there anything else you wish to change?"

"Well, since you ask... I notice we are walking at a leisurely pace. In fact, we are strolling toward the drawing room."

"Yes?"

Lowering her voice to barely a whisper, Caro said, "I always seem to be in a hurry. The bell rings and I have to hop to it."

"So, you would like to stroll."

Caro grinned.

"I don't actually expect you to run."

"Oh, I never said you did. I suppose it's the tone of

the bell. It rings with urgency and one has the instinct to jump into action."

"I shall try to ring the bell with less urgency." Evie hesitated but then found the courage to ask, "Anything else?"

Caro gave a pensive nod. "I think that's all for now."

"So, apart from the concerns you have raised, you enjoyed your meal?"

"Oh, yes. Tremendously."

In the drawing room, Evie gestured toward a set of chairs in the corner.

Accepting a cup of coffee from Wilson, she settled down to ponder the idea of Lorenzo using cocaine.

What could have possessed him to take such a risk and how had he ended up with cocaine contaminated with another substance?

Stirring her coffee, she then thought about the bright young things driving expensive vehicles…

"I think you've stirred that enough," Phillipa said as she took the chair next to her.

"I've been wondering about the price of motor cars. You all drive fairly expensive vehicles. How do you manage it?"

"I borrowed mine."

Evie stopped stirring her coffee. "Is that a euphemism?"

"Certainly not. I'm shocked that you would think me capable of stealing a car. If that's what you meant and I'm sure you did."

"My apologies. I did not really mean to imply… I mean… Well, I'm still cross with you for taking such a callous risk. However, that does not really warrant a lack of trust. I'm happy to hear all about you borrowing a car but, right now, I need to know how the others can afford their vehicles. You said it yourself, Batty hires himself out. That suggests he is in need of money and I assume he doesn't get any from the estate which we know is in disrepair."

Phillipa shrugged. "No one really talks about it but I have heard mention of generous relatives covering debts."

"If we search everyone's motor cars, what do you think we'll find?" Evie asked.

"There's only one way to find out." Phillipa made a move to get up.

"No. We can't go out now. Everyone will notice."

Caro suggested creating a distraction. "I could spill my coffee on you." Leaning forward, she whispered, "I know how to remove the stain."

"Please don't. We'll have to be patient and wait until everyone has retired for the night."

Caro cleared her throat. "You haven't asked what I discovered."

Evie tried to remember the seating arrangements. Caro had been flanked by Lord Alexander Saunders and the young man with ginger hair, Edward Spencer. "Is Alexander's father a duke?"

"Yes. His mother's dowry has kept the estate afloat and in good running order. I didn't get that from him. Earlier, I had a chat with Lark Wainscot and I pretended to be fishing around for a husband. Alexander hopes to find an heiress to strengthen his position, which leaves me out of the running. Unless, of course, you wish to endow me with wealthy relatives."

He might be looking for an heiress but he didn't have any money problems. He would hardly risk becoming involved in anything that might cause a scandal.

Caro cleared her throat again. "Do you wish to endow me with wealthy relatives?"

"Oh… Yes, of course."

"Fabulous. This night is getting better and better." Responding to Phillipa's look of confusion, Caro explained the ruse Evie had contrived. "I never realized I had it in me but I am having tremendous fun pretending to be a lady."

"I'm sorry, I interrupted you earlier. What were you going to say?" Evie asked.

"Oh, it's about Sir Warwick's wife and how she died."

Evie had avoided the awkwardness of asking but had imagined she had succumbed to some sort of illness.

"I found out about it before I became a lady," Caro said. "Most of the downstairs staff have been tightlipped but I managed to get something out of the cook. According to her, Lady Warwick had a riding accident. A car spooked her horse, she fell and broke her neck."

Phillipa and Evie gasped.

They both looked toward the door as the gentlemen, who'd obviously finished their drinks and cigars, joined them in the drawing room.

A thought took shape in Evie's mind. When Sir Richard had stopped by the side of the road to offer assistance, he had been driving from the same direction Isabel and Lorenzo had come from…

Phillipa leaned forward and whispered, "Are you considering the possibility he might be involved in Lorenzo's death?"

"I'd hate to admit it, but as the good detective says, at some point coincidences tend to become suspicious."

Caro pressed her hand to her chest. "Yes, but... Sir Richard has been so hospitable and... I take it he didn't make a fuss about me being both Caro and Carolina."

"No, he's a good sport." Evie finished her coffee and set her cup down. She watched everyone making themselves comfortable. Everyone except Tom and the detective.

Evie waited a few minutes and when they didn't appear, she said, "I wonder if anyone will notice if I suddenly slip away."

"Would you like me to create a diversion?" Caro asked. "I suppose I could spill coffee on myself but this dress is too pretty to ruin. The light shade of pink might make it difficult to fix a stain."

"No, that's fine, Caro. I'll... I'll sneeze." Evie made quite a show of it. "Oh, heavens. I'm afraid getting caught in the rain has given me a chill. I'll have to go upstairs to fetch a wrap."

"That will work too," Caro whispered.

Evie rushed upstairs and rummaged through her luggage. When she didn't find a wrap, she snatched a handkerchief. On her way down, she headed straight for the servants' stairs and went down until she found the kitchen where she asked a footman for directions to the back door.

"I'll light the way for you, milady," the footman offered.

"No need. Do you mind if I borrow your lamp?"

Nodding, the footman led the way. "Be careful. The cobblestones in the yard are uneven and still slippery from the rain. I'll stand by the door, just in case."

"Thank you." The moment the back door opened, Evie regretted not finding a wrap. The breath she drew in chilled her to the bone. Bracing against the unseasonal cold, Evie took care treading across the yard. On her third step, she hit a protruding edge and nearly stumbled.

She could see a light outside the stables and, from a distance, could make out the shape of the motor cars. Drawing closer, she saw a shadow moving. "It had better be Tom or the detective," she murmured under her breath even as she worried about encountering someone else.

Belatedly, she wished she'd taken greater care to see if any of the other gentlemen had been missing from the drawing room.

The person must have seen her coming. The light Evie had seen went out and the stable yard faded into the darkness.

Holding the small lamp out in front of her only gained her an extra foot of light. Regardless, or foolishly… she forged ahead, her eyes straining to see.

Something moved.

Evie tensed and her instinct went haywire. A part of her pushed for a swift retreat to safety while another part, one she barely recognized, urged her to forge ahead.

She took courage and stepped forward but only because she knew the footman had remained by the kitchen door.

The shadow moved again.

Since she couldn't decide if she should retreat or go forward, Evie moved sideways.

She took a couple of hurried steps forward and,

again, she moved sideways. With the stable yard in darkness, she couldn't tell how close she'd come to the motor cars.

"Halt," someone whispered in a hushed tone.

Evie responded by rushing forward.

"Put away your revolver, detective. It's Lady Woodridge."

"Tom?"

"Who else did you think would be out here?"

"I don't know," Evie admitted.

"If you didn't know, why did you persevere?" Tom demanded.

Evie defended herself by saying, "The footman is still standing at the kitchen door. One yelp from me and he would have alerted the entire house."

Tom pushed out a frustration filled breath. "Why did you come out here? You might have alerted the others."

"As if your absence hasn't already done that... Anyway, I had to speak with the detective... About Sir Richard and the way his wife died."

Chapter Nineteen

LIKE THIEVES IN THE NIGHT

"*C*aro, your maid, is parading around as Lady Carolina, your cousin twice removed, and you have engaged her services to question the car rally group?"

While Evie didn't care to answer a question with a question, she couldn't help it. "Detective, that's the part you found intriguing?"

The detective pushed out a breath. "You're right. I should be used to you by now."

"What exactly is that supposed to mean?" She lifted a staying hand. "Don't bother making excuses. You think I interfere. That is absolute nonsense. All along, I have been forthcoming with useful information."

"With all due respect, Lady Woodridge, you do make a habit of bartering for information."

"I think you would be hard-pressed to find someone to fault me in that regard. Anyone in my place would do the same." She held up the lamp and moved toward a motor car. "Why are you standing around in the dark?"

"Our lamp went out," Tom said. "And then you came along…"

"And just as well I did." Evie swung the lamp toward the detective. "So, detective, what do you make of this business? I really don't wish to think Sir Richard has plotted to take his revenge. The fact I have even mentioned this new knowledge shows I am prepared to put aside my personal feelings. Although, I do still harbor reservations. He has suffered a great loss which might have influenced his behavior and forced him to make some bad decisions…"

"I will have to look into the accident report. In order for him to, as you say, take revenge, he would have to know something about the driver responsible. Until I can see the police report, I won't be able to take any steps." He crossed his arms. "In any case, what exactly are you suggesting? Do you think he haunted the road waiting for the driver responsible for his wife's death to appear so he could… force him to inhale contaminated cocaine?"

Grief could be overwhelming and push a person to take extreme measures… "Fine," Evie conceded. "It does sound ludicrous."

"But worth looking into," Tom said. "Remember, there is a gap between the time Lorenzo left Halton House and met his unfortunate end. For all we know, Isabel and Lorenzo might have stopped along the way and… Well, we know Sir Richard had been traveling along the same road." Tom brushed his hands across his face. "Yes, it does sound ludicrous. I can't even begin to imagine what might have happened then."

"I can," Evie chirped. "Stricken with grief, Sir Richard had been waiting a year to exact his revenge.

Let's assume the police report will have details about the driver and let's also assume the police decided the driver had not been at fault. Not convinced and certainly not satisfied, Sir Richard decided to take matters into his own hands. He is a prolific reader and might have come across information leading him to believe Lorenzo was in fact a cocaine user on his way to... Portsmouth. Actually, that might not be so farfetched. Sir Richard might have read about him being in Brooklands... Anyhow, employing the utmost patience, Sir Richard carried with him a contaminated amount of cocaine. Upon meeting Lorenzo on the road, he... Well... you get the gist of it." She knew the police focused on collecting physical evidence and studying the facts but, in her opinion, she saw nothing wrong with considering other possibilities, including wild speculations.

The detective shifted, then he surprised Evie by saying, "My apologies for my earlier behavior, Lady Woodridge. I'm afraid this case has me on edge. So far, there haven't been any solid leads and I feel you are all being put at risk."

"That's why we should join forces, detective. The sooner we have this sorted out, the sooner I can return to Halton House." She hoped he wouldn't let pride stand in his way.

"While you two discuss your differences," Tom said, "I'll see if I can find something in the cars. If you would hold the lamp closer, please..."

Evie smiled at the detective. "Yes, I think we can set aside our differences for the sake of our common goal."

The detective nodded. "Agreed."

"I'll... I'll just stand by and act as official holder of the lamp," Evie suggested.

"Here's something." Tom drew out a parcel from one of the trunks.

The detective had a look at it and then proceeded to unwrap it. "It's a thick layer of fabric wrapped around a package of cocaine."

"Whose vehicle is it?" Evie asked unable to identify it because it had been covered against the rain.

The detective cleared his throat. "Mr. Winchester's. I'd say someone wanted to incriminate you both."

"Thank you for not jumping to conclusions, detective. Is there any way you can get fingerprints from the package?"

"We'll have to wait until tomorrow. With any luck, we might be able to find something. Not that I see it will do us much good since I doubt the perpetrator's fingerprints will be on file."

Could Caro really have overheard the person responsible for distributing the cocaine packages? But why would they put a parcel in Tom's motor car?

"Oh…"

The detective and Tom turned toward Evie.

"I'm sorry. Something just fell into place." As she told them about Caro's observations, she tried to join the dots. Had the parcel been placed in the trunk by the same person who'd tampered with their tire? Why? "Detective. I take my hat off. You deal with devious minds every day. How do you ever manage it?" Another thought struck. "Is the parcel addressed?"

"Hold the lamp closer, please." The detective brushed his hand across his chin. "Portsmouth."

"Phillipa said she received instructions to deliver the parcel," Evie remarked.

"This one doesn't have instructions." Tom shrugged.

"It's possible they intended taking it back once we reached Portsmouth."

Evie gritted her teeth. "Our collaboration has been enlisted by stealth. If this gets back to the dowagers, I shall never hear the end of it."

Tom gave her a pat on the shoulder. "You can put out that fire by using your leverage."

Evie could never confront the dowagers. She didn't have it in her to make a fuss about a few pieces of furniture being removed from the house.

The detective shook his head. "Is this something I need to know about?"

"You already have too much on your plate, detective," Evie assured him. "This is only a small domestic matter." Although, if any of this business became public, Evie suspected her reputation would suffer without any hope of ever being repaired. "I only need to make sure I do not become the notorious Countess of Woodridge." Turning her attention back to the parcel, she asked, "What shall we do with this?"

"I suggest putting it back for now. I will keep an eye on the motor car tonight. Luck is on my side. My room has a corner window which faces the stables." The detective placed the parcel where they had found it and guided them back inside the house.

Evie returned to the drawing room making a show of holding the handkerchief to her nose to justify her absence.

A while later, Tom and the detective appeared, both talking about the game of billiards they'd supposedly played.

"Have I missed anything?" Evie asked as she took her seat next to Caro.

Caro nodded. "I have been following your instructions and studying the car rally group. Having conversed with all of them, I have found it quite interesting to now see how they behave. For instance, when I spoke with Unique, she came across as being quite lively. But I have observed a different side to her. She appears to fall into quiet introspection. Something must be weighing on her mind because a wedge appears between her eyes. Anyhow, the moment someone approches her, she lights up and becomes vivacious."

Evie's eyebrows curved. She would call that a public mask but Caro seemed to be entertaining a different idea. "And what do you make of all that?"

"I believe her true nature is on display when she is quiet. The rest of the time, she appears to adopt a different personality."

"Don't we all do that?" Phillipa asked.

"Cousin Evangeline doesn't. I have always felt she wears her heart on her sleeve."

Smiling, Evie thought for someone who had struggled to accept Tom Winchester, the chauffeur, stepping into the shoes of Mr. Tom Winchester, self-made oilman, Caro appeared to have made an easy transition from maid to cousin, twice removed...

She had only recently lost her chauffeur. Had she now lost her maid too?

Chapter Twenty

"*I*f you insist on talking about the case, all I have to say is that you're the only person to have left the drawing room," Caro observed. "You set off a wave of murmured remarks. I'm sure they were only expressing their concern and heartfelt wish you did not come down with a serious illness."

Or, Evie thought, they might have panicked.

"Also," Caro added, "if there is a killer among us, I doubt they'll do anything tonight. Everyone is engaged in one form of entertainment or other."

"Killer? Who said anything about a killer?" Evie tried to sound mystified.

"Cousin Evangeline, you seem to think me slow-witted." Caro stifled a yawn and only succeeded in setting them all off. "It seems no one wishes to retire. It is well past my bedtime. I suppose everyone keeps gentleman hours, rising at ten if not later."

"Don't look at me," Phillipa laughed. "Born and bred in the middle of nowhere, I had to get up at the crack of dawn and help milk the cows."

"Didn't you have servants to do that?" Caro asked.

"We did, but my parents wanted to keep us honest and learn to appreciate our advantages. I'm not really complaining. Once, my motor car broke down between villages and I had the skills to help myself to some milk."

They both turned to Evie who had been busy taking mental notes of everyone's behavior.

"Cousin Evangeline. Do you have any tales of hardship growing up that I don't know about because we're cousins twice removed and have only now discovered each other?"

Hardship?

For her fifth birthday, her father, who had made most of his wealth in the railways, had engaged an engineer to build Evie a functioning model railway big enough for her to sit on. Yes, she'd been pampered and, some would say, spoiled.

Evie engaged her creativity and said, "One summer, I had to fish for my supper." She made a point of leaving out the part about it being a game. Although, the rules had been strict. Everyone who caught fish then had to sell it, which had been a task and a half since all the neighbors had been as rich as Croesus and their French cooks had been too snooty to purchase fish from the local silver spoon riffraff.

Evie tuned out and glanced around the drawing room. Sir Richard had once again retired early. As had the detective who'd wanted to keep an eye on the stable yard from his window. She couldn't see anyone making a move to call it a day.

Batty and Charlie had invited a couple of others to play cards.

Unique, Marjorie and Lark had procured some

pencils and paper and were drawing portraits of each other.

The others sat around the piano listening to Edward Spencer tinkling with the piano keys. Evie watched the play of light on his ginger hair and wondered if she should make a special trip to a Parisian salon.

Feeling she needed to make more of an effort, she said, "Yes, I do insist on talking about the case because it needs to be resolved. We have physical evidence of trafficking." Now, they needed a motive for murder. Mostly, they needed suspects.

Evie searched for Tom and found him talking with Lord Alexander Saunders.

It took her a few moments to catch Tom's attention. But when she did, he excused himself and crossed the room.

"Have you had a spark of an idea?" he asked.

"I might have. Correct me if I'm wrong, but we seem to be under the impression someone placed the parcel in your trunk the night before we left Halton House. What if we're wrong and someone wanted to dispose of evidence without necessarily getting rid of it? They might have put the parcel in your car today."

"You might be onto something there. I brought out the luggage and didn't see anything. I don't know why I didn't think of it before."

Once again, Evie felt they were playing a waiting game.

Lowering her voice, she said, "I know we should wait for the detective to read the police report, but what if the parcel of cocaine found in Lorenzo's car is different to the others? What will that mean? Had he been in competition with someone else?"

Tom shrugged. "It might mean he worked for someone else or he wanted to take over someone else's territory."

"Is that how it works in the trafficking world?"

"I probably know as much as you do about the subject."

"Phillipa." Evie leaned forward and lowered her voice to a whisper. "Can you think hard about this. You might have seen someone hovering around the vehicles or, like Caro, you might have overheard a conversation that didn't quite make sense at the time."

"At the risk of coming across as flighty and indifferent, I can't say that I ever noticed anything odd about anyone."

They all lifted their eyebrows.

Phillipa added, "Odd as in, out of the ordinary behavior for them."

"What about anyone missing from the group for any length of time?" Evie asked. At some point, they would have to stock up on the cocaine parcels. How did they gain access to their supply?

"It's hard to say." Phillipa shrugged. "Even when we're traveling together, there's always someone bringing up the rear. Sometimes, they fall behind or... they lose sight of the motor car ahead of them and end up taking a wrong turn."

"Yes? Can you think of a specific instance when that happened?"

"I wish I could but no one really pays much attention to what's going on. I'm sure they didn't notice me missing until someone needed to ask me something. I have no trouble picturing someone turning to ask me a question only to realize I wasn't there. It might have taken them a couple of days to decide to do something about it."

They all fell silent. The parcel's intended destination had been Portsmouth. So, the person responsible for putting it in Tom's vehicle had probably assumed Evie would continue on with the car rally group.

Evie had already told Charlie and Batty she would be returning to Halton House.

That put them in the clear. Unless they wanted the cocaine parcel to be taken to safety back to Halton House…

What if someone wanted them to take the parcel to Portsmouth because they didn't want to risk doing it themselves? That would narrow the list of suspects to anyone who didn't know Evie had planned to return to Halton House.

Everyone except Charlie and Batty.

They were once again in the clear.

"If I wanted to throw people off my trail, what would I do?"

"Fade into the background," Phillipa suggested.

"Or," Caro said, "take center stage. Become the life of the party."

Evie had actually been thinking more along the lines of actually doing something…

Caro clicked her fingers in front of Evie's eyes. "Are you still with us?"

"Yes, I lost myself in thought." Charlie and Batty both knew of her plans to return to Halton House. By placing the parcels in Tom's motor car, they would think no one would suspect them.

Now they were back on the list of suspects. Perhaps

they intended collecting their parcel after their trip to Portsmouth…

No, that didn't make sense.

"Now you look confused," Caro said.

Evie wondered if they should let everyone know they were not continuing on with the car rally. It might serve as a prompt to remove the parcel from Tom's vehicle and then the detective would have someone to interrogate.

Nodding, Evie leaned forward and whispered, "Listen up, everyone. I have a plan."

Chapter Twenty-One

SPREAD THE WORD

"I think we should have consulted with the detective before letting everyone know of your plans to abandon the car rally," Tom mused. "And... I'm not really sure I understand your reasoning."

"It's simple. If someone other than Charlie or Batty tries to retrieve the parcel because they now know we are not going to Portsmouth, then I can finally cross Charlie and Batty off the list. It will be a small step but, considering how much time I have spent including them in the list and taking them off, it will, in fact, be a significant step forward."

Caro and Phillipa had moved from one group to the other and had woven the news into the conversations.

Within minutes, the car rally group had, one by one, excused themselves and left the drawing room.

"Does that mean they are all guilty?" Caro asked.

"We'll find out soon enough."

Once they had all left, Evie and Tom made their way to the library to take up their vigil at a corner window. If they leaned out far enough, they could see the stable yard.

"I'm getting a stiff neck," Evie complained.

"Is that my cue to take over from you?"

Evie moved away from her position at the window and flopped down on a chair. "I have abandoned my post. That's your cue." She glanced over at the clock. Nearly midnight.

Tom said, "So far, no one appears to have acted on our open invitation to give themselves away."

Evie laughed. "We were rather blunt about it. In hindsight, if I were driven by selfish reasons, I would try to delay the investigation for at least five days."

"Five days," Tom murmured and then laughed. "I see. You're hoping to be forced to stay here until Isabel's family arrive."

Evie stifled a yawn. "Does that make me devious and selfish?"

"It makes you a survivor."

She'd been that for quite a while, but not in the way the average person would think. Instead of navigating the difficulties that daily life could bring for some, she had to navigate the complexities of a society she sometimes still struggled to understand.

"Earlier, I made up a story about the hardship of having to fish for my supper. In reality, I am one of the lucky few, brought up without a care in the world. Yet, my father always tried to educate us in the ways of the world." Evie laughed under her breath. "He used the most creative ways to make us understand the value of a coin. Also, while I enjoyed a luxurious life, my father also encouraged me to run around barefoot and swim in the lake."

"Are you trying to illustrate a point or are you making light conversation?"

"Both, and I'm trying to keep myself awake. I suppose my point is that, if I had to, I would be able to increase my wealth or at least ensure it is not significantly diminished. From a young age, we were equipped with the necessary skills. It's not something I really need to concern myself with as I am fortunate enough to have a brother I can trust to look after my interests. But not everyone can say that. We know Batty will inherit an estate on its last legs. We also know he has found creative ways to earn a living."

"I thought you had cleared him of all wrong doing."

"It's not exactly my place to do so. In any case, that would be a mistake. He might be a master of disguise, pretending to be hard up when all along he is the head of some sort of trafficking consortium."

"Guilty until proven innocent?"

"Yes, I believe your habit of assuming the worst about people has rubbed off on me." Evie straightened. "He does have the strongest motive to become involved in the trafficking of drugs and I doubt he would be satisfied with earning a small fee for delivering parcels."

"Now you think he's the mastermind?"

"He could be. But would he be capable of killing his competition? Assuming Lorenzo had been working for himself or another band of misfits, he would have posed a threat to Batty's operation. Then, there's Charlie. He is such a jolly character, no one would suspect him of carrying out nefarious activities. What do we know about his family background?" Evie surged to her feet and went in search of the 'Stud Book'. She found a copy of Burke's Peerage in a prominent shelf.

"A bit late in the day to be doing some reading," Tom murmured.

"If Henrietta had been here, I would not have to use this. She knows everyone who is anyone." Evie waved the book. "It lists all peers and their descendants."

"Who will be the lucky first?" Tom asked, his tone conveying a hint of amusement.

"Lord Braithwaite, Charlie to his friends. I believe his joyful manner makes him the least likely suspect." After a lengthy search, she said, "It would appear we were wrong about Charlie being a first-born son. Actually, I can't remember if we even made that assumption."

"Dare I ask?"

"His father is the Duke of Linsborne and the family name is Braithwaite. Charlie goes by the name Lord Braithwaite which makes him a second son because the first son uses his father's secondary title of Marquess of Tiltham."

She heard Tom push out a breath.

"I know, it can be somewhat confusing. You should have been around when I first set foot in an English drawing room. I refused to speak to anyone in case I got the title wrong. My mother hired a Baron's daughter to act as my guide into society but I believe she played a few tricks on me. It didn't take me long to realize there can be nothing more terrifying than addressing a duke as 'my lord' when a social inferior should address him as 'your grace'."

Tom gave her a mock shudder. "I'm having trouble picturing you as anyone's inferior."

"I made a few blunders." She grinned. "But my natural charm won the day."

"So, what do you make of Charlie being a second son?" Tom asked.

"Second and third sons usually have to make their own way in the world. Although, the second son is thought of as 'the spare' and still stands a chance of inheriting. It's rather a tenuous position to be in."

"If you want to know what I think, second sons should receive some sort of compensation for all that waiting around for something that might or might not happen."

"I agree, but then, you and I are American and tend to see things differently. I'm not sure I would be entirely happy if my older brother had inherited everything."

Evie turned her attention to searching for Batty's entry. "Lord Hemsworth is a first born son, but we already knew that. His exact title is the Marquess of Hemsworth and he will, one day, become a duke. Now that I think about it, he actually outranks me. That's a major faux pas. I'm sure I've preceded him into every room."

"It's not something you'll have to worry about if he turns out to be a villain."

She turned the pages, looking for her next person of interest when the sound of a commotion had her rushing to join Tom by the window.

"Did it come from the stable yard?" Evie asked.

"I believe so. Stay here. The detective might need assistance."

"There is absolutely no way on this earth I would stay in the library by myself. I'm coming with you."

Chapter Twenty-Two

TAKE THE BAIT

*R*eaching the kitchen, Tom surged ahead and, finding the back door standing ajar, he burst out onto the cobbled yard while Evie slowed down.

She had no desire to plunge right into the middle of a melee empty-handed. Taking a gas lamp from its hook, she lit it, but before stepping outside, she rushed through the kitchen and located a rolling pin.

"Practical and armed. Henrietta would be proud of me," Evie murmured.

Charging across the cobblestoned yard, she held up the lamp and made out three shapes. Her timing could not have been better. The discord had been settled and, coming closer, she could see the detective and Tom flanking another man.

Lord Alexander Saunders.

She reached the group in time to hear the tail end of an explanation.

"…slipped under my door. I found the message when I retired for the night. You must understand, we have an agreement. No one asks questions."

"Yes, well. I am asking questions now and I expect answers." The detective sounded both determined and annoyed. "Where is the note?"

Evie expected Lord Saunders to say he had disposed of it but, to her surprise, he drew it out of his pocket.

At last, she thought. This could provide a physical lead to the ringleader. Now they only needed to get everyone's handwriting sample.

"Do I need to seek legal counsel?" Lord Saunders asked. While his voice carried a hint of concern, he seemed to have some defiance left in him. Sliding his hands inside his pockets, he lifted his chin.

"We'll discuss this further in the morning," the detective said and dismissed Lord Saunders.

Evie didn't hide her surprise. "You didn't even scold him for taking such a silly risk."

"I would not have stopped you," the detective said.

"I'm not sure I can do that. He might outrank me. In fact, I'm sure he does."

"Would that really stop you, Lady Woodridge?" the detective asked as they made their way back inside the house.

"I suppose not, but don't tell anyone I said so."

Back in the library, Evie studied the note. "This could have been written by anyone. You'd have to bring in a handwriting expert. I assume there is such a profession."

"What do you mean?"

"Look at the handwriting. The letters flow in perfect copperplate script. It could be mistaken for my own handwriting and that cost me hours of arduous labor to perfect under the strict guidance of a tutor who demanded nothing less than perfect imitation of the samples he provided." She studied the paper and noticed the coat of arms on the top. The perpetrator had used Sir Richard's letterhead which could be found in all the rooms.

"I will leave you both to it. I need to get an early start and check with the local constabulary." The detective turned only to stop. "In case it slips my mind, thank you for suggesting we inspect the parcel found in Lorenzo's car."

Evie smiled. "It makes sense to pool our expertise, detective. Mine appears to be developing into a severe case of suspecting everyone."

When he closed the door behind him, Evie sighed. "I honestly don't know how the police ever manage to capture so many criminals. For all we know, my butler might have punctured your tire."

"Edgar? Why would he do that?"

"Because he feels hard done by and is desperate to resume his position at the London house." She picked up the copy of Burke's Peerage. "I think I'll leave this until tomorrow. If I don't try to get some sleep now, I'm afraid today's events will keep me awake all night."

A while later, as she lay in bed, Evie stared into the darkness.

Something felt different.

No maid.

Every night since her arrival at Halton House, Caro had been there to help her undress.

In less than a month, she had lost her chauffeur, her maid and quite possibly, her butler…

"Caro?" Evie brushed the sleepiness from her eyes. "It is you."

"Good morning, milady."

"What happened to Carolina?"

"I thought I might let her sleep in." Caro stopped in the middle of the bedroom and smiled. "There really is nothing to this business of pretending to be someone else. I thought I would find it dreadfully confusing."

"Didn't you play at pretending when you were little?" Evie asked.

"I grew up surrounded by brothers. They were not exactly interested in dressing up and playing make believe games with me."

Evie stretched and yawned. "I spent endless hours daydreaming and pretending to be a pirate princess sailing the seven seas."

"Did anything happen last night?" Caro asked as she selected Evie's clothes for the morning.

Evie had to think hard about the previous night. When she related the story about rushing out to the courtyard, the news didn't surprise Caro. "I'm afraid we are none the wiser."

Caro looked pensive for a moment. "I think if you were to run an illegal operation, you would want to keep your identity secret for fear of reprisals by pretending to be someone you're not."

"You have a cunning mind, Caro."

"Lady Henrietta lends me her penny dreadful novels. I have come to learn a thing or two about evil trickery. It's the charming ones you have to watch out for."

Evie flung the bedcovers off and strode to the window. "I wish I could say it helps to know that, but

I'm afraid everyone I encounter is usually quite charming." Evie knew that came with her position in life. No one would think of being anything but polite to the Countess of Woodridge. "I think you should join us today. We could do with another set of keen eyes."

"You mean it?"

"Yes, of course."

Caro managed to contain her excitement but Evie could tell she couldn't wait to step into the shoes of Lady Carolina Thwaites.

Suitably dressed for the day, they strolled out together.

Before they reached the bottom of the stairs, Evie said, "I think we should focus on the ladies. It's probably a mistake to overlook them."

Marjorie. Lark Wainscot. Unique.

"It looks like a lovely day outside," Caro said.

"You sound worried."

"I didn't bring a hat."

"You can borrow one of mine."

Caro looked away and murmured, "They're too big for me."

Lifting her chin, Evie couldn't help remarking, "I can't tell if you're making a simple statement of fact or if you're trying to say I have a big head. If it's the latter, I'll have to wonder if you also mean to say I might be getting too big for my shoes."

Caro laughed. "Oh, heavens... no. I think I would have said something about your feet being too big."

Before she could stop herself, Evie looked down at her feet. "They are not big. My feet are in proportion to my body."

"If you say so, milady."

Half way to the breakfast room, they encountered the detective.

He inclined his head. "Lady Woodridge." Looking at Caro, the edge of his eyes crinkled, "Lady Thwaites."

"Good morning, detective." Feeling optimistic, Evie asked, "Do you have news for us this morning?"

"Yes, I thought we might meet in the library after breakfast."

Evie took the suggestion in her stride, thinking he would either share everything he knew or distribute information on a need to know basis. "I get the feeling we should have a fortifying breakfast to see us through a busy morning."

They found Tom lingering over a cup of coffee. A few of the car rally group sat at the table. Batty, Marjorie and Lark Wainscot with Edward Spencer joining them as Evie and Caro sat down.

"Unique told me Edward Spencer is an earl's youngest son," Caro murmured. "With three brothers ahead of him. So, no chance of inheriting anything substantial."

Evie noticed Edward smiling at Caro. Arranging some eggs and bacon onto her fork, Evie lowered her voice to barely a whisper and said, "Did you get around to letting others know you are an heiress?"

"Oh, yes. I had tremendous fun with that. It felt like trying on a new dress or taking a vacation."

"I think word might have reached young Edward Spencer. I wouldn't be surprised if he follows you around."

"Oh, you might have to give me a proper country estate or a town house so he can visit."

They were enjoying a second cup of coffee when Sir

Richard took his place at the breakfast table. After a brief chat with everyone, he turned his attention to the daily news.

At one point, Evie thought she heard him murmur his displeasure over the abundance of bad news and the scarcity of good news.

Wondering how they should tackle what little time they had left, Evie thought they should divide and conquer.

Caro had been able to gather some information by having private conversations. Unless the detective could come up with a reason to keep everyone at Warwick Hall, the car rally group would be leaving soon.

Yes, she thought, divide and conquer...

Evie watched the detective to see if he gave anything away. He had said he would contact the constable to establish a few essential facts. His attention, however, remained on his breakfast. The fact he hadn't once looked at Sir Richard could mean anything.

Evie wanted to think he hadn't discovered anything to connect their host to Lorenzo's death. Grief could push a person to their limits and beyond reason. She hoped that hadn't been the case with him.

Glancing around the table, she noticed Lark Wainscot looking at her. They exchanged a smile and before any awkwardness could settle between them, Evie remarked on her rather large brooch.

"It's a unique style. I don't think I have ever seen anything like it."

"A friend made it. It's a three-dimensional homage to the Spanish artist, Pablo Picasso. She assembles all the different shapes made from various materials and overlaps them."

The piece sat on her lapel and Evie could see it pulling slightly on the fabric.

Evie didn't think she would be able to wear such a colorful piece. It contrasted beautifully against Lark's porcelain skin and angular features.

Studying the eye-catching design, Evie remembered Tom saying Lark Wainscot aspired to be a stage actress. She certainly appeared to have the larger than life personality for it.

For such a large piece, the pin would have to be quite sturdy…

Strong enough to pierce through a tire?

The detective cleared his throat and, making eye contact with Tom, Evie and Caro, he excused himself.

They hadn't discussed tactics, but Evie thought it would be best to linger for a while before following him.

"I should like to wear something like it but I'm afraid I wouldn't be able to pull it off."

"Try it on," Lark suggested.

Evie took the opportunity to look at the back of the brooch. "This looks like a strong pin."

Lark nodded. "It's platinum."

Evie had heard of the metal. "The Hope Diamond is set in platinum." Seeing Caro's raised eyebrow, Evie added, "Evalyn Walsh McLean owns it. She's an American mining heiress and socialite. Anyhow, jewelers love working with platinum because of its strength."

Evie placed the brooch against her lapel. That pin definitely looked strong enough to break through the thickness of a tire and Tom had said the incision would have been small enough for it to take a long time for the tire to lose all the air.

Caro leaned in and whispered, "Don't you dare pin

it on. The fabric on your coat is delicate. It won't stand the weight and it will leave a mark."

Looking up, Evie smiled. "Cousin Carolina is ever so fussy about things." She returned the piece just as Tom made his excuses and left the table.

The butler approached her. "Lady Woodridge. There is a telephone call for you."

Evie's heart hammered against her chest. Surprised by her reaction, she pressed her hand to her throat.

The dowagers.

They were the only ones who knew she had taken refuge at Sir Richard's house. Had something happened to them?

She hurried out and, before picking up the receiver, she scooped in a big breath.

Caro, who had followed her, said, "It will be good news. My mother always says we should expect good news."

Giving a stiff nod, Evie placed the receiver against her ear and took the call.

Identifying herself, she listened and nodded several times. Finally, she said, "Yes, I will be there. Thank you for calling."

She disconnected the call and turned to Caro. "The doctor has given the go-ahead for Isabel to leave the hospital."

Sir Richard happened to be walking by and asked, "Is everything all right, Lady Woodridge? Forgive me for saying so, but you look like a damsel in distress."

Evie tried to swallow. Her heart continued to hammer against her chest. She had never worried about the dowagers so she had to assume the last couple of days had taken their toll.

"It's Isabel Fitzpatrick. I mean… Bianchi…" Evie berated herself for not feeling overjoyed by the news of her recovery. "She is ready to leave the hospital." And, going by the relief she had heard in the doctor's voice, he could not have been happier to see Isabel go.

"Caro, could you please alert Edmonds. I'll be needing the car in a moment."

Chapter Twenty-Three

IT IS BETTER TO RISK SAVING A GUILTY PERSON THAN
TO CONDEMN AN INNOCENT ONE - VOLTAIRE

The library, Warwick Hall

Thinking the detective had kept them in suspense long enough, Evie walked into the library and demanded, "Is Sir Richard innocent?"

The detective smiled. "That is the wrong question to ask."

"Do I get three guesses? Be careful how you respond, detective. If you say yes, you'll have to listen to me prattling on…"

The detective pressed his lips together and then pushed out the words. "Lorenzo did not drive the car which spooked Lady Warwick's horse. He'd been out of the country at the time."

Caro nudged her. "I would have loved to hear you prattling on."

"In fact," the detective continued, "the police were never able to identify the driver, which makes them even guiltier for leaving the scene of the accident without notifying anyone. A local farmer witnessed it from a distance and could only describe the vehicle as small and possibly black or burgundy."

The information should have satisfied Evie. However, her rather farfetched idea of Sir Richard haunting the road and seeking vengeance gained momentum.

Evie got up and paced around the library.

Everyone in the county would know Sir Richard. He would have the confidence of every tenant in the area. What if he had come by information the police hadn't been able to access? The authorities would have investigated the matter but they might have missed someone. Evie imagined an estate worker or a local tenant farmer providing Sir Richard with knowledge of a particular motor car being spotted in the area.

She shook her head and decided she needed to let it go. Sir Richard would have passed the information on to the police. She wanted to believe it. She had to.

"There's also the other matter." The detective cleared his throat. "It seems your suspicions were right, Lady Woodridge. Lorenzo's packages do not have an address and it is not wrapped in anything other than paper."

Meaning, he had been in business for himself and... "His competitor killed him."

"That is an idea we are prepared to work with. As you know, Lorenzo Bianchi had been under surveillance. However, we were never able to connect him to anyone of interest."

Evie didn't comment. She had nothing to say. In fact, she would have struggled to voice an opinion.

Nibbling the tip of her thumb, she wondered how long it would take for Isabel's parents to arrive.

Swinging around, she stared at Tom and the detective just as a footman entered the library and made a beeline for Evie.

"There is a message from the hospital, milady."

Heavens. What now?

"The doctor wonders if you could please hurry up. Begging your pardon, milady. I know the good doctor and he... he sounded... Well, not quite himself."

"He has probably come down with a bout of Isabel Fitzpatrick." She thanked him and, turning to the others, said, "I'm sorry. You'll have to excuse me." She rushed out of the library.

Caro trailed behind her and Evie heard her say, "You must excuse her ladyship, I mean... Cousin Evangeline. Lorenzo Bianchi's wife has such an effect on her, she cannot think straight."

Evie kept her gaze fixed on a point just ahead of her. She moved with purpose, her mind fixed on the idea of just getting this over and done with. Along the way, she managed to notice a couple of people in the spacious entrance hall.

"Evie," Tom called out as he tried to catch up to her. "What is going on?"

Evie laughed and then she frowned. She had no reason to laugh. Had the prospect of driving to the hospital to collect Isabel sent her over the edge? "Edmonds is driving us so you don't need to worry. You should go back and get as much information from the detective as you can. I believe he is in a talkative mood."

"He's at his wit's end," Tom said. "If he doesn't find a solid lead, he'll have to let everyone go."

Evie had a good mind to set herself up as a suspect. That way, she would be forced to stay at Warwick Hall and avoid taking Isabel back to Halton House.

Caro tugged her sleeve.

"Yes, we should go." Evie hurried her step only to be tugged back again by Caro.

"I heard it again. The voice."

"Pardon?"

"It's done. But she or he didn't say that this time."

"When did you hear it?"

"Just now," Caro said.

"Did you match the voice to the person?"

Caro shook her head. "No. I... I was trying to keep up with you and hear what Tom had to say. The voice just sort of mingled with all that."

"And you're sure you recognize it as the same voice you heard back at Halton House?"

"Absolutely."

Evie looked over her shoulder and saw Charlie and Batty at the bottom of the stairs. Charlie looked relaxed as he leaned against the balustrade while Batty had one foot on the first step and appeared to be frozen in mid motion.

She swept her gaze across the hall and saw a couple of other people. "I really don't have time for this now. Who knows what Isabel will do if I don't show up soon," she said as she stepped out of the house. "Do you think you could hover around and try to eavesdrop on conversations?"

"Yes, absolutely." Caro swung around and returned to the house.

Evie made a beeline for the waiting motor car. When Edmonds closed the door, she leaned against the window and called out, "Tom. You can't let anyone leave. Drive on please, Edmonds."

The Duesenberg rocked back, stopped and then took off.

"Apologies, milady," Edmonds said.

Evie caught Edmonds glancing at the mirror several times. She brushed her hand across her brow and only then noticed her frown.

Heavens. She must look a fright and with good reason. She didn't know what to expect. She knew Isabel had a survivor's pragmatic outlook, but after claiming someone had killed Lorenzo, Evie couldn't even begin to imagine what she would do.

Would she seek vengeance on the person responsible for killing Lorenzo? And how would she go about it?

Suddenly, Evie couldn't get to the hospital fast enough.

Isabel had only told her someone had killed Lorenzo but, now that she had made a full recovery, she might have more information.

"Step on it, Edmonds. We don't want to keep Isabel waiting."

Edmonds smiled. "Certainly, milady."

Chapter Twenty-Four

RESCUE MISSION

*A*pproaching the small village hospital, Edmonds leaned forward. "I believe they are waiting for you, milady."

Yes, Evie could see the doctor and a couple of nurses with Isabel appearing to address each one like a commander issuing orders to the troops.

"Heavens," Evie murmured. No wonder the doctor had sounded out of sorts, she thought.

Even as the motor car stopped in front of the entrance, Isabel continued her delivery of what would no doubt be strict instructions.

Wanting to put the doctor and his nurses out of their misery, Evie hurried out of the vehicle. "Isabel." When she didn't respond, Evie realized she must have whispered the name so she tried again.

Seeing her, the doctor appeared to almost sink to his knees with relief. He stepped forward, his hand extended. "Lady Woodridge. How very good to see you."

"I came as soon as I could," Evie said, her voice lowered. "How is she?"

"Eager to move on."

"Do you have any instructions? Does she require any special care?"

"Oh, no. Mrs. Bianchi… or rather, Miss Fitzpatrick, is made of sterner stuff."

She had decided to be a Miss again?

Was that even possible?

A nurse hurried forward carrying a suitcase. Edmonds helped her load it up in the car and the nurse scurried off back inside the hospital, grabbing a hold of the other nurse and tugging her along with her.

"Heavens," Evie couldn't help exclaiming again.

The doctor had turned and quite possibly seen the nurses making their escape.

"Yes, well… Miss Fitzpatrick, I believe you will now be in safe hands."

Isabel gave the doctor a bright smile. "If I suffer a relapse, I'll be sure to contact you."

"Oh, but I'm sure you will be far away from here. There are bound to be other doctors in the vicinity." The doctor stepped back. Inclining his head slightly, he swung on his feet and disappeared back inside the hospital.

"You're looking much better, Isabel." Evie guided her into the motor car and settled down beside her. "Drive on, Edmonds." She sat back and tried to clear her mind for a moment before tackling the difficult task. Her questions might open fresh wounds, but she would have to risk it. However, Isabel had other ideas. Clearly, she fully intended to move on.

"Funeral arrangements will have to be made. My poor Lorenzo didn't have any close family. They all perished in the war. I shall have to travel to Tuscany to close the villa. Did I tell you about the Tuscany Villa? It is wonderful but so very far away. I doubt I'll ever have time to visit. I have a suitcase, as I'm sure you noticed. The rest of my luggage is back in London at the Automobile Club. So, I shall have to make do with what I have until I can meet up with my family. They're coming over. Did you hear? Yes, of course you would have heard. I don't know what I'll do without him, but I'm sure someday soon I'll look back and think I worried unnecessarily. You'll have to tell me how you managed after your husband perished with the Titanic. I will have to do better because I will certainly not spend two years in mourning. He would not want that for me and I am far too young…"

Nicholas? Perished with the Titanic? Why did Isabel insist on persevering with that story? Evie did not bother correcting Isabel. She tried to imagine Nicholas rolling his eyes but he hadn't been the type to do so.

Evie estimated Isabel had talked for ten minutes before finally stopping to draw breath.

When Edmonds turned off the main road and onto the road leading to Warwick Hall, Isabel straightened.

"Where are you going? I know this road. We have traveled along it so many times, this isn't the way to Halton House…"

Evie explained the situation, saying the weather had forced them to stay on for longer than anticipated. "Sir Richard has been a marvelous host."

"Well, of course. You are a Countess. That has to mean something…"

Evie waited for an opportune moment to ask about

Isabel's declaration. While Isabel continued to talk about the helpful suggestions she had offered to the doctor and his staff, somehow, Evie managed to switch off and think about Caro hearing the person's voice again.

Evie had seen Charlie and Batty talking together. As for the others hovering around the entrance…

She closed her eyes and tried to remember. She had cast her eyes around but she had been in a dreadful hurry to get to the hospital and rescue the doctor.

The brooch.

Yes. She'd seen it and that meant Lark Wainscot had been there. Evie gave a small nod. She then remembered Lark had been standing with Edward Spencer. She confirmed it with another nod as she also remembered glancing at his ginger hair.

Tapping her hand on the seat she tried to recall who else had been hovering around…

Someone had walked across and blocked her view but that had only been for a few seconds.

Marjorie.

Yes, definitely Marjorie. She had actually been swinging a golf club and she had been talking. Evie remembered seeing her lips moving so she must have been walking across to meet with someone.

Had that been the voice Caro had heard?

Isabel tapped her hand. "Evie? You're miles away. Should I repeat what I just said?"

"Oh, no… That's fine. We should be there in a few minutes."

"So, who else is staying at Warwick Hall? I remember seeing a man with you."

"Oh, That's Tom Winchester." Could she claim to

have known him since childhood? The cover story had worked until now… "I always travel with him. He's… he's a great driver and I haven't learned to drive yet. I'm not even sure I want to learn to drive." Before Isabel could ask for details, Evie went on to say, "What exactly did you mean when you said someone killed Lorenzo?"

Evie had recently learned Isabel could be silenced by the shock of an accident. Quite a feat for someone compelled to speak at breakneck speed from the moment she got up in the morning.

Now she knew an awkward question could be just as effective.

Isabel's eyes fluttered and she leaned back.

Heavens!

"Isabel? Are you all right?"

"Oh… Yes, I'm fine. What happened?"

"I think you might have experienced a brief relapse."

"Yes, the doctor warned me that might happen. He also said… I might talk in my sleep. Perhaps that's what you heard."

No, Isabel had been fully… sort of fully conscious.

"Isabel, did anyone else visit you in hospital?"

Isabel's hand fluttered to her chest. "Oh, no. I don't know anyone here. I mean, other than you."

"Are you sure?"

Isabel looked away and, after the longest pause without saying anything or even moving, she gave a reluctant nod.

Chapter Twenty-Five

A footman must have alerted Sir Richard of their arrival. As the motor car drew closer to the entrance, Evie could see him standing by the door.

"The man has impeccable manners," Isabel remarked. "He doesn't even know me and yet he is ready to welcome me to his castle. What's it called again?"

"Warwick Hall."

Isabel's silence during the last few minutes of their drive had made Evie uneasy. She should have welcomed it. Instead, she couldn't help thinking Isabel had been coerced into silence.

Did she fear some sort of reprisal from Lorenzo's killer? Indeed, had the killer made contact with Isabel?

Bringing the motor car to a stop outside the front entrance, Edmonds jumped out and opened the passenger door. Evie stepped out of the motor car and turned to assist Isabel but Sir Richard rushed forward, extending a welcoming hand.

"Mrs. Bianchi. Please accept my condolences for

your loss. A dreadful tragedy. I hope we can make you comfortable at Warwick Hall. The household staff will be at your service."

Evie watched as Isabel lifted her chin. Knowing her as well as she did, Evie knew if she had been mulling over a problem, she had just dismissed it, making a swift recovery as she regaled Sir Richard with her most charming smile.

"You are a knight in shining armor, Sir Warwick."

"Richard, please."

"And you may call me Isabel."

Sir Richard swept Isabel inside, leaving Evie to ponder the power some women seemed to hold over men. She only had the briefest moment to herself when Caro rushed out of the house.

"Well? Did she say anything more?"

Still struggling to understand Isabel's change of mind, Evie gave a slow shake of her head. "She recanted her story."

"What do you mean?"

"If she said anything, she claims it happened in her sleep and she has no recollection."

"She must be hiding something," Caro said.

"I agree." Evie folded her arms and looked away and across the lush green lawns. "Isabel wouldn't allow herself to be intimidated. I only hope the detective has better luck interviewing her." Deciding she needed to stretch her legs, she said, "Let's walk and talk."

Caro had been busy eavesdropping on everyone's

conversations. "I could not have imagined it. I know I heard the same voice again."

"What were they talking about?" Evie asked.

Caro nibbled on the edge of her lip. "I'm so sorry, milady. I only really heard the voice. As I said, I'd been trying to keep up with you and to hear what Tom was saying. When the voice registered in my mind, the person must have stopped talking. I looked around and all I could see were groups of people chatting. Or rather one person talking and the other listening."

At least the car rally group were all still here. "Why haven't they left?"

"I heard the detective say the circumstances called for everyone's cooperation. Sir Warwick agreed saying he felt invested in the investigation and needed to see it through to completion and find out who the culprit is. Otherwise, he would have to devote his entire life to scouring the newspapers every day looking for news updates. If you ask me, I think he rather enjoys the company."

They reached a conservatory and stopped to admire the plants and fountain with a jolly looking cherub balancing on top.

"On our way back," Evie said, "I tried to remember who else had been standing in the hall. I'm sure I saw Marjorie making her way toward someone." At the time, Evie had been entertaining too many thoughts and everything she'd seen had jumbled in her mind.

As they continued on their way, Caro grabbed hold of her arm. "I wish I could read lips."

"Why?"

Caro pointed to the conservatory. "Sitting by the

fountain. That's Lark and Edward. They look quite serious."

"I don't blame them. Their car rally has been completely derailed."

"No, there's something about them. Look at Edward. He looks different. Almost as if he were standing taller and I think he looks commanding. I might not be able to hear what they're saying, but I would bet anything he is talking business. The late Earl used to look like that. He always reminded me of a cat. Relaxed one moment and, the next moment, quite alert."

"Yes, I think you're right. Looking at how they're behaving now, I can see there's a huge contrast to how they've been behaving in the drawing room."

Caro had noticed that the previous night.

And even on the first day, Evie remembered seeing Lark participating in the human pyramid and finally collapsing from laughter.

They rounded the conservatory and came up to the French doors leading to one of the drawing rooms. Walking close to the windows, they saw several people inside. Everyone appeared to have broken up into groups of two.

"It's almost as if they are all conspiring to make us suspicious of them," Evie murmured.

Caro harrumphed. "If you ask me, the detective went too easy on them."

"Would you have suggested he use medieval methods to extract false confessions?"

"That's extreme, but he could have yelled. I haven't heard him raise his voice."

"I have," Evie said. "In fact, he became quite cross

last night with Lord Alexander Saunders. He had a right to be. The handwritten note Lord Saunders showed him could have been written by anyone. The bait he'd set only provided another dead-end."

"At least he now knows someone is orchestrating it all."

They continued on and came up to another drawing room. At a glance, Evie didn't see anyone, but then someone inside moved and she realized Isabel sat on a large comfortable fainting couch with Sir Richard sitting beside her.

"That's an interesting picture," Caro said. "What is the age difference between them?"

"I'd say about twenty years." She knew Isabel's age but she had only estimated Sir Richard's. "Are you suggesting they have formed an instant connection?"

Caro nodded. "It's been known to happen."

True. She had fallen in love with Nicholas the first time she'd seen him. "They are both vulnerable," Evie mused.

Caro agreed. "More reason for them to form an attachment."

Evie shivered. "If it leads to something, that would mean living within driving distance of Isabel. I would never get any rest, peace or quiet." Evie shook her head. "I shouldn't fret. Her family will be arriving soon and I'm sure they will insist she return with them."

"Would you really begrudge her the joy of finding someone so soon?"

"No, of course not. Although, I wish she could be happy somewhere else."

As they walked away, Evie couldn't help looking over her shoulder and working on a contingency plan. Being ever so pragmatic, Isabel might wish to move on and find someone else as soon as possible. If she did, Evie could suggest she hold onto the Tuscany house and make that her home base.

"I see all the motor cars are still here," Evie said.

They'd reached the stables. Lifting her hand to shield her eyes from the sun, Evie saw a couple of people standing by the cars. One of them appeared to be Tom.

The detective emerged from the house and headed toward the stables. Noticing them, he stopped until Evie and Caro caught up with him.

Evie asked, "Detective. Have there been any new developments?"

"Not as such, certainly not what you hope to hear, Lady Woodridge. A couple of the cars have been tampered with. It must have happened during the night. I've had a long chat with the stable hands and no one heard or saw anything."

"Tampered with? In what way?"

"One has a leak. Another one had all the engine oil drained out of it."

She looked toward the house. "It looks like someone wishes us all to stay here."

"Are you about to suspect Sir Richard?" Caro asked. Or one of his household staff, Evie thought. According to Sir Richard, they were all overjoyed to have people staying at the house.

"I'm sure Sir Richard had nothing to do with it."

"Are they repairing the vehicles?" Evie asked.

"They're doing the best they can. A mechanic has been called in from the village but he hasn't arrived yet." The detective brushed his hand along his neck. "I believe we might all have to remain here for a while longer."

Evie studied him for a moment. "Detective. If I didn't know better, I would suspect you of forcing everyone's hand."

Glancing at Evie, he gave her an innocent look. "Do you really believe I would be desperate enough to do that?"

"Yes, and I'm only sorry I didn't think of it myself." Evie looked toward the stables. "I trust you've kept yourself busy this morning."

The detective nodded. "I had a few telephone calls to make and I've been actively observing everyone. I suppose I still live in hope someone will put a foot wrong."

"So, you'll know if everyone stayed within the grounds of Warwick Hall," she said.

"Why do you ask?"

Evie told him about Isabel changing her mind and insisting she had not been aware of saying Lorenzo had been killed.

"You think someone visited her and issued a warning?" he asked.

"You must admit it sounds suspicious." Evie nodded. "Isabel had been so adamant…" Evie shrugged. "Then again, she had just suffered a tremendous shock. I had hoped she would be able to provide us with more detailed information."

A spark of an idea had Evie smiling.

"I can tell you are entertaining an idea. Would you care to share?" the detective invited.

"I'm not sure I should."

"Oh, no," Caro exclaimed. "Please, don't keep us in suspense."

"It's not exactly a brilliant idea and I'm sure you will all disapprove... But, here goes. We could use Isabel as bait."

Chapter Twenty-Six

Warwick Hall library

"Miss Fitzpatrick felt fatigued and has retired for a rest," Sir Richard said when Evie found him in the library.

"You are most kind to continue to allow us to stay, Sir Richard. This must be a dreadful inconvenience."

"Nonsense. This is all proving to be quite entertaining. I'm overjoyed to see your friend so determined to move on. She spoke at great length about her husband, expressing the strongest sentiments for him. She tells me he would have wanted her to celebrate his life rather than dwell on her loss. I find her attitude truly admirable and quite remarkable for someone so young." He uncrossed his legs and made a move to get up only to sit back again. "You know, she mentioned going to Tuscany and how she is not accustomed to traveling alone. I wonder if you might advise me on something. I would like to offer my assistance and accompany her on her travels. Do you think she would be amenable to the idea?"

Evie had no doubt that had been Isabel's intention all along. She never did or said anything without reason. Which made her wonder why she had thought Evie had perished with the Titanic.

"Isabel would be delighted."

"You don't think it would be inappropriate. She is, after all, insisting on reinstating herself as a Miss."

Evie suspected that wouldn't be for long. "Not at all."

He gave a pensive nod. "I have sent a telegram to her family. They are already well on their way and I wished to set their minds at ease." Sir Richard checked his watch and got up. "Would you like me to ring for some tea? I'm told the others have congregated in the drawing room for morning refreshments. I'm on my way over to join them."

"Thank you. I'll go along in a short while. But before you go, I wonder if you might be able to help me."

"Ask away," Sir Richard invited.

"Would you be able to find out if anyone organized to send a letter?"

"Certainly. My butler, Wilson, will know." He turned to leave only to stop. "I'm curious… Is this related to the investigation?"

Evie gave a small nod and hoped Sir Richard would be satisfied with that.

He mirrored her nod and left the library to join the others for morning tea.

Evie felt compelled to think Isabel's altered version

of what she'd said did not spring out from out of nowhere. Someone had put pressure on her...

Indulging in a few moments of quiet, she closed her eyes and hoped to refresh her thoughts but Isabel's changed attitude continued to plague her.

Sir Richard had suggested everything had started at Halton House.

What if it had?

While Evie would prefer to avoid any association to illegal activities that would in any way bring disrepute to the name of Woodridge, she had to be realistic and trust she could deal with the aftermath.

Evie sat back and stared into empty space. According to Phillipa, during the first round of interviews, the detective had been keen to know what Lorenzo had talked about during his brief stay at Halton House.

"All along, the detective has been harboring suspicions and trying to find a connection to the car rally group," Evie murmured.

As Phillipa had been present during Isabel and Lorenzo's chat with everyone, Evie had tried to place everyone who had been in the drawing room at Halton House.

But the mental image she'd drawn couldn't provide her with what she really needed.

Phillipa might have seen something and not realized it. Perhaps a hand gesture or someone signaling with their eyes... Exchanging a look with Lorenzo.

"Our dear detective must think Lorenzo knew someone within the car rally group," she whispered. Someone who had then gone on to betray him.

As much as she felt she needed some quiet time, Evie

wished she hadn't encouraged Caro to stay in the stable yard with Tom. She could have tossed around some ideas with her.

Looking around the library, Evie decided she needed to make a list. Equipping herself with pen, paper, and the copy of Burke's Peerage, she settled down in a comfortable chair by the window where she could occasionally look up and rest her eyes on the scenery.

She had already found a few names in Burke's Peerage but there were some others she hadn't finished investigating.

Lord Alexander Saunders.

From memory, he stood to inherit a dukedom, which made him a first-born son. Frowning, Evie tried to remember who had shared that information with her.

"Caro." And she'd found out about Alexander's background from… "Lark Wainscot?" Yes, Evie remembered Caro had then asked if she could be an heiress. Frowning, Evie tried to remember the details of that conversation. Had Caro said Alexander stood to inherit?

After half an hour, she conceded defeat. "I can't find anything." Setting the book down, she looked out the French doors to the garden beyond.

She saw a couple of people stride by on their way to the drawing room, including Caro who stopped to make a few hand gestures signaling she needed a cup of tea.

Lark Wainscot and Edward Spencer emerged from the woods and they too made their way to the drawing room.

She resumed her search and, this time, focused on Edward Spencer. Sifting through her memory, she thought Caro had mentioned he had a title but he didn't stand to inherit. Why didn't he use the title?

"An Earl's third son. He could definitely use extra money."

Looking at her list, two names stood out.

Batty and Edward.

One needed money to restore the estate he would eventually inherit and the other needed money simply to survive because with two other brothers ahead of him, he didn't stand a chance of inheriting.

She underlined the names and wrote, "Motivation. They would both be driven by need but what would compel one of them to commit murder?"

More need, she thought and then added, "Greed."

Tom had alluded to the possibility of Lorenzo invading someone's territory to traffic his own cocaine…

She then wrote down Lord Alexander Saunders' name.

She hadn't been able to find his name in Burke's Peerage…

Why would he pretend to have a title?

Looking around her, she huffed out a breath. "The detective has spoken with everyone, Evie. It's his job to find the culprit. And, until he does, he is going to keep us all here."

Evie surged to her feet and made her way to the stables where she found Edmonds tinkering with the cars.

He removed his cap. "Milady."

"Where's Tom?"

"He went inside in search of you."

"Have you made any progress with the vehicles?"

He slanted his eyes one way and then the other, possibly to make sure no one could hear him. "We are doing our best to… assist the detective."

Meaning, he and Tom were stalling for time.

"Didn't the detective send out for a mechanic from the village?" Evie asked.

Edmonds grinned. "He did, milady. I guess the mechanic must be busy."

In other words, the mechanic wouldn't be coming any time soon.

When Edmonds continued to grin, Evie said, "There's something you're not telling me but you wish to tell me because you find it ever so amusing."

He once again looked around to make sure no one could hear him.

"As a matter of fact, milady…" He leaned in and whispered, "There is nothing wrong with the cars. The detective only asked me to make it look as though there is so I spilled some motor oil and temporarily removed a few essential pieces."

"It seems the detective is more devious than I gave him credit for." Evie tapped her chin. "Edmonds. Caro told me you heard noises in the night at Halton House."

"Yes, milady. But I didn't see anything or anyone."

"Did you see Lorenzo Bianchi and his wife arrive at Halton House?"

"Yes, milady. When they went inside, I had a closer look at his car. A real beauty. I would have loved to look at the engine but I didn't dare."

"Did you happen to see them leave?"

He nodded. "I had a view of the entrance, milady."

"When they left, were they alone?"

When he hesitated, Evie wondered if he had understood the question. "Did anyone walk out with them?"

Edmonds smiled. "I believe so, milady."

"A man or a woman?"

"Both. There were several people to see them off." Edmonds brushed his hand across his chin. "Now that I think about it, as they got in the car, someone else approached the driver. A woman. They had a brief chat and then she stepped back."

It's done.

Had Caro heard the woman saying that after Isabel and Lorenzo had left?

---

Chapter Twenty-Seven

*E*vie knocked on Isabel's door. Not wanting to get caught up in conversation in the drawing room, she'd had to hunt down a maid to direct her to Isabel's room.

When she didn't hear a response, she tried again, eased the door open and slipped inside.

She found Isabel curled up on a chaise lounge, gazing out of the window.

"Oh, I thought I heard a knock. So lovely of you to come and see me. Sit. Make yourself comfortable. I hope the others don't think I'm being rude. I suppose they'll understand. Oh, heavens. What they must think of me. I've been wondering if I should go down and force myself to be the life of the party. Richard tells me they are all quite lively. Then again, I saw them at your house so I've seen it all with my own eyes. Although, they were captivated by Lorenzo so I might have seen a toned-down version of them."

When Isabel finally stopped to draw breath, Evie

snatched the opportunity to say, "I wanted to ask you about your visit to Halton House."

Isabel gave her a brisk smile. "Oh, you mustn't worry about me thinking you were rude not to be there. I promise I won't tell a soul. Although, Emily Post made it plainly clear. It is rude for a hostess to be out when guests arrive. Perhaps you missed that chapter…"

Belatedly, Evie realized Isabel might have put two and two together and realized she had avoided the encounter on purpose.

"Do you remember anyone approaching Lorenzo to have a private word with him?"

"Let me think. He had such a larger than life personality, everyone wanted to be around him. You would think I'd be jealous, especially when women flocked around him but I knew he only had eyes for me."

Evie persevered. "Do you remember a woman approaching him as you were leaving?"

Isabel stretched her arms out. "Heavens. Everyone came out to wave us off. For a moment, I thought they might form a guard of honor and then run alongside the motor car."

Evie leaned forward. "Think, Isabel. This is important."

"There might have been. I'm not sure…"

Why would Isabel choose to be evasive? "How did you know we had headed out this way?"

"Lorenzo asked, of course." Isabel pressed her hands to her cheeks. "Heavens. You are full of questions today and I'm afraid I'm not myself, not yet. That's why I retired to my room…"

Realizing she wouldn't get anything out of Isabel,

Evie got up and strode to the window. She had to find a way… Ask the right questions. Or threaten her…

"There are penalties for withholding information from the police."

~

It did not surprise Evie to discover Isabel did not respond well to threats. Certainly not empty threats from Evie. But someone had issued a warning to Isabel. A threat serious enough to secure Isabel's silence.

Evie found Caro in the drawing room sipping a cup of tea and seated next to Tom. A brief glance established everyone else's presence.

"I'm going to have to put myself on a slimming diet," Caro said as she helped herself to another piece of cake. "Sir Warwick's cook makes the most delectable cakes. I can't stop eating them."

"Is this all you've been doing? Eating and drinking tea?" Evie helped herself to a cup and sat next to Caro.

"Tom and I have been comparing notes and have both noticed everyone casting glances our way. I think they're onto us. Meaning, they suspect that we suspect."

Evie lowered her voice and told them about her conversation with Edmonds.

Nodding, Caro said, "I remember seeing the motor car driving off. I'd been looking out of your bedroom window and…" Caro gasped. "Now that I think about it, I think I saw someone lingering by the front steps. A woman. Yes, a woman. She wore a skirt."

"Can you recall anything about the color of her clothes or her hair? Anything that might help to identify her?"

"Give me a moment. It will come to me, I'm sure." Caro looked around the drawing room. "Everyone seems to be favoring a combination of black and white today." She tapped her chin. "Beige. As in, a day out boating or playing lawn tennis. Does that help?"

"Yes, thank you." Now, Evie had to remember who had been wearing what at Halton House on the morning she and Tom had trekked out.

"We could search everyone's luggage," Caro suggested. "Tom could be a lookout and warn us if someone comes."

Evie nodded. "Yes, fabulous idea. Where's the detective?"

"I believe he went into the village to consult with the local constabulary," Tom said.

"Why do I suddenly feel we have been set up as bait?" Evie murmured. Left alone to stir things up, she thought.

"Whatever happened to using Isabel as bait?" Caro asked.

"I…" Evie couldn't remember. Had she been side-tracked?

"I suppose it didn't feel right." Caro set her tea and cake down. "We should avoid attracting attention so I will go up first. If I linger, I'm afraid I won't be able to tear myself away from that cake."

"I suppose the detective is convinced one of the car rally group is responsible," Evie whispered.

"He hasn't exactly shared his reasoning," Tom explained, "but I believe you're right. He's onto something. I think he has some detectives asking questions in town about people's backgrounds."

"Where in town?"

"He mentioned the Automobile Club. He wanted to know if any of the car rally group went there."

Evie's cup rattled on its saucer. "Has he sent someone out to Halton House?" She could have spared him the trouble. "Someone did approach Lorenzo. I just spoke with Isabel and I am more certain than ever someone has tried to silence her. She never misses an opportunity to prattle on and yet, when I asked about the people they came into contact with, she clammed up."

"So, you think she's hiding something."

Evie nodded. "Edmonds saw a woman approach Lorenzo before he left Halton House and Caro just said she witnessed it from the upstairs room. Yes, absolutely. She is hiding something. I'll even go so far as to suggest she is afraid."

Sir Richard approached them.

"Lady Woodridge. I have asked my butler about any messages sent out and he told me he delivered one to the hospital. Unfortunately, the envelope had been left in the entrance hall table. So, he is not able to tell us the identity of the sender. I hope that is of some help to you."

"Thank you, Sir Richard. That is most helpful."

"I shall make further inquiries with the staff. Someone might have seen a guest carrying an envelope."

As Sir Richard moved away, Evie murmured, "This has to be a lead. In fact, it's probably the first one we have. Proof someone here is responsible for Isabel's silence."

Evie and Tom spent a few minutes observing the car rally group.

Intrigued, Evie asked, "Are they playing a game?"

"Yes, I believe it's the word game, hangman. You know, for every wrong letter guessed, a body part is drawn hanging from the gallows."

"Oh, yes. My brother loved that game." Evie shivered. "They are obsessed with murder. Did you know, in the 1700s, criminals sentenced to death by hanging were occasionally given the opportunity to play the game? The executioner would pick a word. If the criminal guessed the letters in the word, his life would be spared. In a cruel twist of fate, many of the criminals of the time were illiterate." Shaking her head, Evie added, "Here's another tidbit. Some people were hung for receiving stolen goods."

"Are you suggesting we line them all up and march them off to the gallows for inadvertently trafficking in cocaine?"

"I said no such thing."

"But you entertained the thought."

Evie shrugged. "I'm still cross with Phillipa. She's not gullible." Evie tapped her chin. "Maybe she's trying to fit in and that's why she didn't question finding a parcel in her trunk with instructions to deliver it. Now that I think about it, they might all be trying to fit in." Evie checked her watch. "I should go up. You could go out the other door and meet me at the bottom of the stairs. We were serious about needing a lookout."

"You mean, a stooge." Tom set his cup of coffee down. "What exactly are you hoping to find?"

"A clue. Some sort of physical evidence of wrongdoing or involvement." Also, Evie hoped Caro would identify the skirt the woman who had approached Lorenzo had worn. "I'm surprised the detective hasn't already checked everyone's luggage."

"He meant to but," Tom said, "unlike you, he didn't think of sneaking around. He needs a couple of constables at hand to keep an eye on everyone."

"I don't see any point in waiting for him."

"So, you won't take offense when he catches you meddling?" Tom asked.

"I'll try to remain impervious. Besides, I'm sure he'll forgive me once he learns of our progress. Someone here is responsible for scaring Isabel into silence."

Tom chortled. "You haven't seen the contents of the letter. Someone might have wanted to express their condolences and convey their best wishes for a swift recovery."

Chapter Twenty-Eight

*E*vie met Caro at the top of the stairs. "We'll have to be methodical and quick about it."

"I assume we're looking for a piece of clothing I can identify. What else?" Caro asked.

"Anything. Something to link someone to Lorenzo's death."

Tom appeared. "I thought you were meeting me at the bottom of the stairs."

"Did I say bottom? I'm sure I meant the top of the stairs. Now that you're here, let's work on our signals. If you see someone coming… walk by the door and knock."

"And what will you do?" Tom asked, his tone amused.

"We'll figure something out."

"They won't come up," Caro said.

"You sound confident."

Caro sighed. "No one ever returns to their room after they have gone down in the morning. If they need anything, they send their maid or valet and if they don't have one, they send a house maid. Everyone knows they need to allow the maids access to the rooms so the beds can be made and the rooms cleaned."

"Oh." Evie looked and sounded surprised.

Caro chortled. "Are you telling me you were not aware of the unspoken rule?"

"I don't wish to contradict you, but last night I came to get my own wrap."

Caro tilted her head. "And is that what you would normally do?"

Evie looked askance. Normally, she would have asked a footman to pass on a message to Caro. "My maid had been otherwise occupied playing the role of Lady Carolina."

"Are we going to do this?" Tom asked.

Caro and Evie nodded.

Inside the first room, Evie said, "This must be Marjorie's room. I remember seeing her with a golf club." She pointed to one resting against the bed.

"Now that we are actually doing this, I feel awkward," Caro admitted. "It's an invasion of privacy."

"Relax. I've done this before and we are well justified, Caro or is it Carolina? By the way, that is a pretty dress."

"Yes, I've often admired it on you. Just as well I packed some extra clothes for you." Caro held up a small leather-bound notebook. "It looks like a diary or some sort of itinerary. She has the name of villages listed along with numbers. I assume those are distances traveled."

Evie searched the drawers for pen and paper. "Make a quick note of some of those dates and places. We'll pass the information on to the detective and he can see if they make sense." She looked over Caro's shoulder. "Is there any mention of Lorenzo?"

"None that I can see at a glance," Caro murmured. "Have a look while I search through the wardrobe."

Evie flipped through the pages. "By the way, do you remember if you heard the person remark 'It's done' before or after Isabel and Lorenzo left."

"After."

"You didn't have to think about it. Are you sure?"

Caro nodded. "After I watched their departure from your bedroom window, I made my way along the gallery. That's when I heard the remark. Everyone had been making their way back inside." Caro grumbled under her breath. "Nothing here."

They moved on to the next room.

Seeing a headband she recognized on the dresser, Evie said, "This is Unique's room. I remember the headband."

Caro picked up a couple of photographs. "It's the car rally group."

Studying one of the photographs, Evie said, "Am I imagining it, or is Lark Wainscot always with Edward Spencer?" They stood together and slightly apart from the group. Tapping her chin, Evie added, "There's something else I wanted to ask you. Did Lark Wainscot tell you Lord Alexander Saunders had a title?"

"Yes. He will inherit a healthy estate but he still wishes to find an heiress."

How odd, Evie thought. "Lark seems to have gone into great detail. Yet, I couldn't find his name on Burke's Peerage."

"Is there such a thing as a new title?" Caro asked.

Evie gave it some thought. "Occasionally but rarely,

new titles are formed but they are usually bestowed upon a member of the royal family."

Caro set down the photographs. "Why would Lark lie about Alexander having a title?"

Why indeed…

"To think," Caro continued, "I might have been duped into marrying him."

"I'm sure his lack of title would have come up during the marriage contract."

Caro giggled. "I suspect I might have taken the ruse that far. I really am having tremendous fun being Lady Carolina."

The door to the room opened a nudge.

Evie and Caro froze. Then, exchanging a panicked look, Evie grabbed hold of Caro and pulled her down and toward the bed.

Down on all fours, they again exchanged a look of panic before scrambling to take cover under the bed.

Evie heard the light footsteps moving across the room. Then silence as the person walked over the rug. They would have to wait until the person left the room.

She hadn't done something like this since she'd played hide and seek with her brother…

What if they didn't leave the room?

Caro clutched Evie's hand. They both held their breaths, their eyes widening as they saw a pair of feet approaching the bed.

"Hello?"

Caro grumbled. "It's Phillipa." She crawled out from under the bed, straightened and helped Evie to her feet. "You startled us."

Grinning, Phillipa said, "Tom warned me I might

catch you in the act. Did you really think you could hide under the bed?"

"Where else would you have suggested?" Evie gave her a lifted eyebrow look. "What are you doing here?"

"I noticed you all left the drawing room. I hope that doesn't mean I'm some sort of suspect."

Looking at Evie, Caro said, "Perhaps Phillipa knows if Lord Alexander Saunders has a title or not."

"It's never really come up." Phillipa shrugged. "No one ever really uses their title unless they need to in order to secure a roof over our heads."

"Well, Alexander is not listed in Burke's Peerage. Why would Lark Wainscot make it up?"

"She's an actress. She's always making things up."

Evie laughed. "The same could be said about most of the people in the group. Especially those wishing to become writers."

As she rummaged through Unique's wardrobe, Caro said, "Nothing beige here. Unique favors bold colors with patterns."

"Great." Evie turned toward the door. "That's another person off our list. Let's find Lark's room." Just as Evie turned the doorknob, she heard voices. Tom's and someone else's.

Isabel's.

Evie pressed her finger to her lips calling for silence and pressed her ear to the door.

After a moment, she turned to the others. "Isabel needs some fresh air."

She eased the door open a fraction and checked to make sure Isabel had moved on.

When she turned to say they could proceed, something caught her eye.

A hat sat on a small trunk. Evie strode toward it and examined it.

"What are you looking at?" Phillipa asked.

"The hat pin. Would you say this could be used to pierce through a tire?"

"Yes, with some effort."

Caro giggled. "Milady, I believe all the ladies in the car rally group have now become suspects. At this stage, you're supposed to cross people off the list, not add names to it."

"Thank you for pointing that out, Caro." Evie set the hat down. Turning, she swept her gaze across the room and, as she did, she looked out of the window. "Is that Isabel?" She appeared to be walking at a brisk pace. Every few steps she took, she looked over her shoulder and then hurried her step.

"Would someone like to volunteer to go after Isabel and make sure she doesn't come to any harm?"

Phillipa took a step back while Caro looked away and tried to avoid Evie's gaze.

"I take it neither one of you wishes to be landed with the task."

"She's your friend," Caro whispered.

"Fine. I'll go after her and you two can search Lark's room."

Chapter Twenty-Nine

*E*vie tried to be as discreet as possible, leaving the house unnoticed. She strode at a sedate pace, looking up, shielding her eyes to catch sight of a bird sweeping across the sky. Yes, she thought, anyone seeing her would think she had gone out for a stroll and a breath of fresh air.

By the time she had stepped out of the house, she had lost sight of Isabel. Evie hoped she hadn't gone far.

Ten minutes into her walk, she thought she spotted her. Evie hurried her step and called out her name.

Another few minutes and she finally saw Isabel sitting in the folly, leaning against a column, her legs tucked under her, a handbag on her lap.

Where had she planned on going?

She didn't look too happy to see Evie. In fact, she didn't even bother to lift the edge of her lip.

Did this have something to do with her loss? Had it all finally sunk in?

Evie considered apologizing for the intrusion.

Instead, she sat beside Isabel and patted her hand. "Your folks should be here soon."

"Yes, I daresay, they will be." Slipping her hands inside the large pockets of her coat, Isabel tipped her head back and sighed. "They'll expect me to return with them, but that is not going to happen." Brightening, Isabel sat up and gave a firm nod. "There is too much to do and see here."

"Of course, you've grown used to traveling and constantly moving around. But where will you go?"

"Lorenzo and I were recently in Monaco. I made a ton of connections there. He met up with friends who wish to set up a race. It's going to be a big affair. Then, there's Italy. We were there last year. Again, we met so many people, I won't have any trouble getting around. Even if I returned to America I doubt I'd be able to sit still in New York or Rhode Island. Lorenzo and I traveled all year round, from one race to the other."

"Did you plan on returning to America with him?"

"Not for a while. He wanted to stay in England. When he heard Brooklands had opened again, we headed here."

"Had it been closed?"

Isabel nodded. "During the war and then for repairs."

"Where were you before you ended up at Brooklands?"

"North of England. I loved it. We drove from one town to the other and all the villages in-between, up and down, across and then back again. It felt like a honeymoon. Just the two of us."

Had Lorenzo been distributing his cocaine? Had he then found a new distribution route when he went to

Brooklands? A route already covered by the car rally group? Although…

They had also been distributing in the north of England. That's where Phillipa had been, while the rest of the car rally group had been driving around the south of England.

Isabel sat up and adjusted her hat.

Evie looked at her as she continued to think about the possible connection to trafficking. She focused on Isabel's hat. It had an upturned brim, like a sailor's hat…

Evie frowned. She'd seen a similar hat recently.

Had it been a hat?

Evie leaned back against the column. No, not a hat. A sailor's top with a skirt that had actually been wide legged trousers. Cream colored. The sort of outfit one might wear on a sunny day out boating.

Huzzah!

Evie felt a rush of excitement even before the full picture took shape in her mind.

Surging to her feet, she said, "I suppose you came out here to have some peace and quiet. I'll leave you to it."

"Wait a minute. I know that look. You just had some sort of idea and… and… Did I say something? I'm sure I didn't."

"I'll see you back at the house." Evie took off at a trot. She knew she needed to wait until the detective returned, and she would but, in the meantime, she could tell the others.

"Stop," Isabel called out.

Hearing the desperation in Isabel's voice, Evie slowed down long enough for Isabel to catch up to her.

"Whatever you are going to do, don't. You can't."

"What do you mean?" Evie asked, her voice full of innocence.

"You've figured something out. I know you've been trying to get some sort of information out of me just because... because I said something silly."

"I'm sure I don't know what you're talking about."

"You've been asking me if I remember someone approaching Lorenzo. Now you've somehow figured out who it is. You can't do anything about it. Let it go."

"Whatever do you mean?"

Isabel grabbed hold of Evie and pulled her back. "She's dangerous."

"She killed your husband. Don't you want justice?"

"She'll kill me too. She said she would."

"Did you know?"

Isabel tugged her back.

"Isabel. Did you know what Lorenzo was doing?"

"They threatened his life if he didn't do it," Isabel cried out.

"Who's they?"

"I don't know."

It sounded as if the detective would have bigger fish to deal with. Evie shook her head. "She needs to be stopped." Evie broke free and, in the struggle, she nearly lost her shoe.

Isabel grabbed her again and for a moment, Evie thought Isabel would wallop her with her handbag.

"You can't," Isabel growled.

The ground remained slightly soggy from the recent rain, so Evie used that as an advantage to gain some leverage. When she broke free again, she turned the tables on Isabel and, grabbing hold of her, pulled her along.

Despite the tug of war, they managed to get to the house just as a car sped past the porticoed entrance to Warwick Hall, presumably headed toward the gates.

"That's her," Evie bellowed.

A second later, Tom's roadster sped by. Evie saw him hunched over the steering wheel in hot pursuit.

Seeing this, Isabel loosened her hold long enough for Evie to drag her back to the house just as Caro burst out through the front door.

"She nearly killed us," Caro yelled.

"What?"

"She came up and, when she saw Tom standing outside her room, she pulled out a revolver. Phillipa and I had just searched her room and we were coming out to share our find with Tom." Caro held up a small bottle. "We found this. Tom says it's the sleeping powder used with the cocaine."

"Where's Phillipa?"

"She's trying to contact the detective. Tom told her to try the local constabulary."

Evie looked one way and then the other before she made the firm decision and headed toward the stables.

"Where are you going?" Isabel demanded.

"I'm going to follow them."

"But you don't know how to drive," Caro called out.

Evie picked up her skirt and put more effort into reaching the stable yard. Seeing her chauffeur, she called out, "Edmonds, start the car." Glancing over her shoulder, she saw Isabel and Caro catching up to her.

"I'm coming too."

Isabel yelped. "So am I."

They all jumped inside the Duesenberg.

"Step on it, Edmonds."

"As you wish, milady."

"When I said step on it, I actually meant, really step on it. Go as fast as you can."

"Certainly, milady." Edmonds cleared his throat. "Hold on to your hats, ladies."

"They have a head start," Caro said. "We'll never catch up to them."

When they sped by the gatehouse, Evie expected Edmonds to slow down and try to decide which way to turn, but he now appeared to be possessed by the idea of driving fast.

As if reading Evie's thoughts, Edmonds remarked, "I just saw a flock of birds in the distance taking flight, milady. I assume they were startled. They have most likely gone this way."

They all looked out the windows.

Sure enough, birds were taking flight.

Caro tapped Evie on the shoulder. "I take it you figured out the identity of the woman."

Evie nodded.

"How?" Caro asked.

"Isabel's sailor hat."

"Yes, very pretty. But, what about it?"

"It reminded me of the sailor outfit Lark Wainscot wore on the first day when Batty introduced everyone. I suppose you found out when she pointed the revolver at you?"

"No. Along with the sleeping powder, I came across the skirt in her wardrobe only to realize the skirt was actually a pair of wide legged trousers. We were on our way over to tell you."

Lark Wainscot.

Keeping her eyes on the road ahead, Evie wondered if they'd made a mistake. Everyone in the car rally group had been taking orders from someone to deliver parcels.

Someone had been determined to keep their identity a secret.

What if the woman Caro and Edmonds had seen approaching Lorenzo had merely been the messenger?

Caro cleared her throat.

"Is something on your mind?" Evie asked.

"What if we're wrong?"

"I have just been entertaining the same doubt." But they couldn't be wrong. "It's not just the skirt that identified her as the woman who approached Lorenzo. I think she's also responsible for tampering with Tom's tire. On the first night, Batty asked about my involvement in a recent murder case and Lark Wainscot showed a great deal of interest."

Someone in charge of trafficking drugs wouldn't want Evie around sticking her nose where it didn't belong.

Caro laughed. "I'd forgotten she pointed a revolver at us. That, more or less, gave her away."

"We'll soon find out." Evie pointed ahead. "Is that them?" Why were they slowing down? "Edmonds. You need to slow down too. Remember, she has a revolver." Evie hoped Tom remembered that too.

Edmonds smiled. "I didn't think she'd get far. I took out a few essential parts out of some of the motor cars, and others had most of their gas emptied out."

"I see another motor car up ahead. That's why

they've slowed down." Caro cheered. "It's the police. They're blocking the road."

"What is she doing now?" Evie craned her neck but the road had dipped slightly so she couldn't see clearly, especially as Tom's car kept getting in the way.

Edmonds cleared his throat. "I believe she is trying to turn."

Caro gasped. "She's heading straight for Tom."

At the last minute, Tom swerved out of the way.

"Fabulous. Now she's headed straight for us." Caro ducked. "Tell me when it's over. I can't watch this."

When she saw Edmonds steer the motor car toward the shoulder, Evie reached for the steering wheel and adjusted it.

"Milady?"

"Our car is bigger. If she tries to steer out of the way, you get in front of her. I doubt she'll keep going much longer. You said she doesn't have much gas left."

"She might have enough," Edmonds whispered.

Tom had turned his motor car and had set off in pursuit again with the police now closing in.

Noticing Isabel had been unusually quiet, Evie turned and saw her staring straight ahead, her eyes not blinking, her face pale.

Caro peered out from the back seat. "My goodness. She's still heading our way." Caro pressed her hands to her face but Evie could see her peeking from between her fingers.

"She's holding steady, milady. I think she's challenging us."

Evie narrowed her eyes. "Heavens. She's aiming the revolver at us. Everyone, get down." Evie's voice hitched as she called out, "Swerve, Edmonds."

Everyone dived for cover.

Everyone except Isabel.

Edmonds sunk into his seat but he managed to get the Duesenberg to swerve away from the oncoming motor car.

"Stay down, everyone."

Evie's shouted command lingered for a moment only to be drowned out by the report of a revolver echoing around them.

Chapter Thirty

Silence settled inside the motor car followed by an eruption of frenzied questions.

"Who's been hit?" Caro demanded. "Please tell me it's not me."

As Edmonds straightened and brought the Duesenberg to a stop, Evie swung back to look at Isabel.

She looked quite content and calm.

"Isabel?" Evie's gaze dropped to her lap.

A revolver?

Out of the corner of her eye, she saw Tom's car drive by, followed by the police. She then saw Lark Wainscot's car limping to a stop.

"Um, why does Isabel have a revolver?" Caro asked.

For the first time, since climbing into the car, Isabel responded with a smile. "I always carry one and I'm quite a good shot, if I do say so myself."

Evie had found Isabel's earlier silence disturbing. The calmness she heard in her voice now stunned her.

Isabel looked over her shoulder at Lark Wainscot's vehicle and shrugged. "She got what she deserved."

Caro gasped and swung around. "Did she… Did she kill her?"

"No." Evie's voice sounded flat. She scooped in a breath. "She got the tire."

Isabel's smile widened.

"I take it Lark Wainscot is the woman you were too afraid to identify," Evie said.

"That was then, this is now. She gave herself away."

They all watched as Tom and the police rushed toward Lark's motor car. The police had their weapons drawn. Tom, thank goodness, stepped aside to let them do their job.

"What will happen to her now?" Caro asked.

"I suppose the police will take her into custody and question her."

To her credit, Lark Wainscot did not put up a fight.

Evie straightened and looked ahead. Something didn't feel right. Why would she try to make a run for it? All this time, she had managed to keep her identity secret…

Caro had said she'd found the sleeping powder in her room but anyone might have had that in their possession for their own private use.

Lark Wainscot could have talked her way out of it. She could have made something up. Why hadn't she?

Edmonds cleared his throat.

Evie nodded. "I suppose we should return to the house. We could all do with a cup of tea."

Wilson, the butler, stood back and watched them all filing into Warwick Hall.

"I see we are short one guest. I missed all the excitement," Sir Richard remarked as he met them in the hall.

Unable to find any words of explanation, Evie left Caro to fill in the gaps for Sir Richard.

Lark Wainscot had been escorted to the village where she would be placed under police custody and questioned.

Isabel retired to her room saying she'd had enough excitement for one day.

Hearing the sound of tires crunching on the gravel, Evie turned and saw Tom's roadster pull up.

After a few moments, he climbed out of the car and made his way inside. As he strode toward Evie, his eyes pinned on her, she tried to read his stern expression.

"Did you feel it absolutely necessary to follow us?" he asked.

Evie lifted her chin. "We followed at a safe distance."

"And what were you planning to do when Lark Wainscot headed straight for you?"

Tom didn't need to know she had ordered Edmonds to stay on course. "As you can see, we're alive and well."

His eyes narrowed. "You were lucky."

She didn't need reminding. "Someone needs to tell the others. You've drawn the short straw."

Pushing out a breath, Tom went into the drawing room to break the news to the car rally group. When he finished, he turned to Evie. "If you need me, I'll be in the stable yard."

Accepting a cup of tea, Evie watched as everyone fell silent. Either out of loyalty to Lark or from utter disbelief that she could have been in any way involved.

Phillipa rushed into the drawing room. When she

spotted Evie, she hurried toward her and threw her arms around her.

"Everything happened so fast. I had to call the police and then I couldn't get my car started so I couldn't follow you. You have no idea what it's like waiting to hear news."

"Actually, I do. You seem to forget we were both in the same boat not long ago when Henrietta wouldn't let us set foot outside the dowager house when the police were running around the village looking for the killer." Evie signaled toward the door and whispered, "Meet me in the library." She set down her cup of tea and worked her way to the door.

In the library, she picked up the copy of Burke's Peerage and skimmed through it.

Why had Lark made a run for it? Evie's mind failed to yield any worthwhile ideas. She tried to settle down but she couldn't stop fidgeting.

What if…

"Someone told her to run," she murmured. Someone in the group had been issuing instructions. What if they thought the detective had been getting closer to finding the ringleader?

Evie sat up. "They would create a distraction."

Edward Spencer and Lark Wainscot had been constant drawing room companions. Had they been plotting together or had Lark been listening to instructions and carrying them out without question?

When Phillipa strode in, she took the chair opposite Evie. "You look uneasy."

"That's because I am." Evie looked at the copy of Burke's Peerage. Huffing with frustration, she set it down. "I am obsessing about Lark lying. Why would she need to lie about Alexander's title?"

"She might have been having a quiet moment," Phillipa offered. "No one in the group is keen on quiet moments of reflection. So, they create their own entertainment. She probably wanted to amuse herself."

Really?

Evie sat back and tapped her chin in thought. "But... Everyone knows him by his title."

Phillipa laughed. "If I decided to call myself the Countess of Champagne, everyone would go along with me." Phillipa leaned forward. "You're not convinced this is over."

Evie shook her head. "Before I start pointing fingers of suspicion, I really should wait for the detective to question Lark."

"And I should be taking notes for my Countess X mystery books."

"Are you going to make her a masked sleuth?"

"Well, you don't exactly go around promoting yourself as a sleuth. In fact, you made a point of denying it."

Evie got up and paced from one end of the library to the other.

Phillipa said, "Unlike you, I'm relieved this is finally over."

"Is it?"

"Lark is in custody."

"I'm sorry. I can't stop thinking about it. I wonder what it takes to become a trafficker? I'm guessing you'd need financial backing. Do you think Lark has money?"

"She could be working for a bigger fish. In a roundabout way, we were all doing that," Phillipa said. Laughing, she added, "It would be amusing if Sir Richard turned out to be involved."

Evie managed a laugh. "I already suspected him, ungrateful guest that I am."

Phillipa continued, "He said his sons are abroad. Perhaps they're involved in organizing the trafficking."

The door to the library opened. The detective removed his hat and made his way to the couch.

"Detective? Here already?" Evie gave him a minute to settle down before asking, "Did you get a confession out of Lark Wainscot?"

"I certainly did. And I think you know that already," he said. "She didn't even wait to get to the police station."

Surprised, Evie said, "She is pleading guilty."

He nodded. "She even admitted to damaging your tire."

"Did she say why she did it?"

"She killed Lorenzo because he wanted to take over her territory. As for your tire, she'd heard of your involvement in a previous case and worried you might catch on to what they were doing. She wanted to scare you into returning home."

Evie grinned. "She gives me too much credit." Sitting down again, Evie sighed. "I'm not convinced of her guilt."

After a brief silence, the detective said, "No, nor am I." He brushed his hand across his chin.

Evie couldn't hide her surprise. "You actually agree with me?"

"I've never known a criminal to be so co-operative. Not unless they had something to gain and we haven't offered her anything in exchange for information."

Evie couldn't believe Lark Wainscot would be prepared to go to prison for someone else. There had to be a mastermind behind it all.

She turned to Phillipa. "The first time you found a package in your car with instructions, did you tell anyone about it?"

As she shook her head, Phillipa's cheeks colored slightly. "I feel so foolish now. I've since spoken with a few of the others and none of them thought to question it when they found packages with instructions. Don't get me wrong, we're all aware of what goes on. We just didn't think what we were doing had anything to do with drug trafficking. It simply never occurred to us."

"Phillipa."

"Yes?"

"Despite Lark being taken into custody, is there anyone in the group you might suspect? I'm thinking her imprisonment might have thrown light on the matter and sparked off your suspicious nature."

"I don't really have a suspicion nature," Phillipa admitted. "Let me think…" Phillipa clasped her hands together. "I couldn't even take a wild stab at it. What about you? You've mentioned Edward Spencer but I honestly don't see him as the mastermind behind a drug trafficking business. He loves music and poetry. I might even go so far as to say he has a gentle, sensitive soul."

Evie brushed her hands across her face. Isabel had been threatened into silence. However, when the time had come, she had stepped up to the plate and she'd taken action. What would it take for Lark Wainscot to realize how much trouble she had landed herself in? Admitting to killing a man would send her to the gallows. She had to know she would pay for her crimes with her life.

The detective looked down at his hands and cleared his throat.

Both Evie and Phillipa turned their attention to him.

"Edward Spencer was seen at the Automobile Club a few weeks ago. Lorenzo Bianchi stopped there for lunch before going on to Brooklands."

"Are you saying someone at the Automobile Club gave you that information?"

The detective nodded. "One of the waiters finally talked."

"And he saw Lorenzo with Edward?"

"No. But it's enough to know they were both in the same place. It's too much of a coincidence."

Evie crossed her arms. "Are you going to question Edward Spencer again?"

"That's why I returned to Warwick Hall, but I'm giving him some time to get comfortable and think Lark Wainscot has convinced us of her guilt." The detective looked at Phillipa.

Phillipa shot to her feet, her tone carrying the indignation she obviously felt, "I think I know what you're thinking. No, I will not warn him. Yes. You can trust me. However, I am having a difficult time believing Edward is in any way involved."

"He's the least likely person to be involved," Evie reasoned. "The fact you believe him to be innocent proves how well he carries his disguise." Getting to her feet, Evie said, "I'm going to stretch my legs."

"Please try to remain within sight of the house," the detective suggested.

"Yes, of course." And, along the way, she wanted to find Tom and start making plans for their return home.

"I'm coming with you," Phillipa said. "You'll be my alibi, just in case the detective decides I am not to be trusted."

Chapter Thirty-One

"YOU SHOULD STUDY THE PEERAGE, GERALD. IT IS THE ONE BOOK A YOUNG MAN ABOUT TOWN SHOULD KNOW THOROUGHLY, AND IT IS THE BEST THING IN FICTION THE ENGLISH HAVE EVER DONE!" OSCAR WILDE (A WOMAN OF NO IMPORTANCE)

Seeing Phillipa looking somewhat downcast, Evie asked, "Will you continue on with the car rally? If you're not up to it, I want you to know you are always welcome to return to Halton House with us."

That cheered her up. "Oh, yes. I've been trying to work up the courage to ask if I could spend a few days there. This business has left me feeling slightly shaken."

The more the merrier, Evie thought.

"Oh, wait. You want a buffer between you and Isabel."

Grinning, Evie said, "Well, there is that. Although, I'm not sure what her plans are. Either way, I think we both win. You get a roof over your head, and I get to enjoy your company. I might also need you to help me with the dowagers."

"Are they making your life interesting?"

"That's an understatement, but… yes. I think they're doing their best to keep my attention engaged."

"Perhaps they're afraid you might tire of life in the country."

"You might be right. It hadn't occurred to think they might wish to make sure I stay. They know I have a choice and I can live wherever I wish to live." And she had chosen to settle at Halton, but only after being away for two years.

Turning into the stable yard, Evie saw Edmonds but not Tom.

"I have been restoring the motor cars back to working order," Edmonds said. "The detective has asked me to fix them. Mr. Winchester went back inside looking for you, milady."

"Have you had a break?" Evie asked.

Edmonds wiped his hands on a rag. "A cup of tea would go down nicely, milady."

"Well, make sure you go in and get one."

As they continued on their walk, Phillipa said, "It must be lovely working for you. I don't think I would be suited to a life in service, but if I needed to work in a house, I believe I would consider myself quite fortunate to work for you."

"I think you'll find most people try to ensure their servants are content."

They walked on in silence but it didn't last.

"I don't see Edward Spencer as the mastermind behind this trafficking business." Evie shook her head. "He exposed himself by being seen at the Automobile Club. It doesn't make sense." She stopped and turned toward the house. Seeing someone disappear into the stable yard, she tugged Phillipa. "That must be Tom. Let's go see what he's up to."

"It's not Tom," Phillipa said.

They found Lord Alexander Saunders looking under the hood of his motor car.

Their footsteps alerted him of their presence and he straightened. "Lady Woodridge. You had quite an adventure this morning."

"Yes, but it's all been resolved now. You must all still be in shock."

He slipped his hands inside his pockets. "No one ever suspected anything. We can't decide if we should abandon our car rally or surge ahead to take our minds off everything that's happened." He looked around him. "Most of us are feeling restless so I came out here to check on my motor car. Everything appears to be in fine working order."

Evie smiled. "Phillipa and I couldn't sit still. That's why we came out here. I'm afraid I've been wearing out the carpet so I understand your need to find something to do. In fact, I have been so frustrated by this business, I've even tried to lose myself in Burke's Peerage." She took a moment to study his reaction but he didn't even flinch. "Even after all these years of living in England, I am still intrigued by all the titles."

He laughed. "You know it's full of errors."

"Is it? Actually, now that you mention it, I spent some time looking everyone up and I don't recall finding your name."

He gave her a whimsical smile. "I have only recently come into the title. Or, rather, my father only recently came into the title. He never really stood a chance of inheriting but then the war took its toll on his distant cousin's family… the one with the title. They all perished. I suppose the information will be included in the next edition."

He lowered the hood and rounded the motor car.

Evie looked around the stable yard. "It looks like all

the motor cars are ready to go now. The police never did discover who tampered with them."

"I suppose it could have been a prank," Alexander said. "In fact, I'm inclined to believe that."

"Why?"

"Because there was no real damage done."

"Who is your driving companion?" Evie asked. "I noticed everyone drives in pairs."

"I don't," Phillipa murmured.

"I drive alone," Alexander said.

"Is that by choice?"

Grinning, he said, "I like to drive in silence and that's impossible with this group. They're all chatterboxes."

In other words, Evie thought, everyone could account for their driving partner's whereabouts. They all had alibis. All except Lord Alexander Saunders.

Evie made a move to return to the house only to stop. "Something's been bothering me... The detective just told us Lark Wainscot confessed to giving Lorenzo cocaine laced with a sleeping powder, but how did she know Lorenzo would come to Halton House?"

Alexander shrugged. "Perhaps she'd been ready just in case he ever showed up somewhere... some time during our travels."

That would have required carrying the cocaine around with her at all times. The explanation reminded Evie of the far-fetched theory she had contrived about Sir Richard.

Had Lark issued an invitation?

Evie turned to Phillipa. The car rally group had come looking for her at Halton House because, according to Batty, they had known Phillipa had last been at Halton House.

How had Lark known Lorenzo would visit unless she had made sure he would?

Evie checked her watch. "I suppose we'll be leaving soon, but I know if I don't get an answer, I will toss and turn. I'm going to ask the detective. He might oblige me and try to get the answer from Lark."

They managed to take a couple of steps before Lord Alexander Saunders said, "Lady Woodridge."

Evie turned slightly and caught sight of the revolver in his hand.

"Oh…"

He smiled. "I'm afraid you have forced my hand."

"You didn't come out here to check on your motor car. You came out to make your getaway."

"I'll only need a few minutes. If anyone asks, they have been instructed to say I went into the village to purchase gas for everyone." He nudged his revolver toward the stables. "Would you care to join me inside?"

"May I ask why?"

"Because I need to lock you up. I'm sure you will be rescued in time. There is always someone in the stables. Now, be quick about it." He nudged his revolver again.

"I'm ever so relieved to hear you won't be using that weapon." Taking hold of Phillipa's hand, Evie walked toward the stables. She trusted the police would eventually catch up with Alexander, so she had no intention of trying anything foolish. "Did Lark know you had mixed the cocaine with sleeping powder?"

"Not at all. I asked her for some, saying I'd been having trouble sleeping. Otherwise, she was none the wiser. As far as she knew, the little satchel contained a sample of our product to entice Lorenzo into distributing it."

Evie felt relief for Lark. She might not have to face the gallows…

"Did you tell him to come to Halton House?"

"An associate of mine informed me of your encounter with Lorenzo and his wife. I couldn't let the opportunity slip by."

"Are you really a Lord?"

Opening the door to a storeroom, he laughed. "As a matter of fact, yes, I am. The story I told you is quite true. Alas, the estate has drained all the funds that came with the inheritance. As you know, it is not appropriate for a gentleman to seek gainful employment but I needed to inject money into the estate." He gestured with his revolver.

"This won't end well for you. You haven't thought this through. Even if you manage to get away, you won't be able to resume your life."

"That's perfectly fine. I'm not the first born. In a twist of irony, I am not doing this for myself." He pressed his revolver against the small of Evie's back.

"You can't seriously think you'll get away."

"I suppose this is not the time to say I'm afraid of the dark," Phillipa murmured.

The storeroom door closed and they heard the key turning.

"Hold my hand. Nothing is going to happen to you."

"There might be spiders in here. I've never told you, but we have some nasty looking spiders back home. Quite deadly…"

"Let's cross our fingers and hope someone finds us soon. In fact, we don't really need to rely on providence.

Edmonds will be here after he's had his cup of tea and I'm sure Tom will come out looking for me." They heard the sound of the motor car rolling away. "Any minute now…"

A while later, Phillipa murmured, "I've never been any good at judging the passing of time, but I suspect we have been locked up here for a lot longer than a minute."

"I am inclined to agree with you." Evie pressed her ear to the door only to jump back. "Ugh. Cobwebs."

Phillipa shrieked and threw her arms around Evie.

"You're squashing me. And why are jumping up and down?"

"To lessen the chance of a spider climbing up my leg."

"If there are any spiders in this storeroom, they are now cowering in a corner."

"How can you be so calm?"

Evie pressed her hand to her chest and tried to calm her thumping heart. "I'm not, but since we don't know when we'll get out of here, I think we should try to reserve our energy."

A sliver of light appeared on the floor.

"I think someone just came into the stable," she whispered.

"Why are you whispering?" Clearing her throat, Phillipa yelled for help.

The key on the door turned. "Lady Woodridge." Edmonds stepped back. "How did you get in there?"

Evie and Phillipa rushed out of the storeroom. Then they took turns to look at each other's back to make sure there were no spiders crawling around.

"It's rather a long story, Edmonds."

Phillipa huffed out a breath. "Did no one notice us missing?"

Evie then noticed Tom standing behind Edmonds. "Mr. Winchester. Did you come searching for us?"

"Yes, it felt too quiet so I knew there had to be something wrong and then I noticed you were nowhere to be seen."

"We have no idea how long it's been since we were locked up in that storeroom. Lord Alexander Saunders must have made his escape by now."

"He tried. The police took him into custody ten minutes ago. They'd taken the precaution of barricading the roads."

"Are you saying the detective expected this to happen?"

Tom shrugged. "He hoped he might be able to flush out the real culprit but he thought it could have gone either way. I guess Lord Saunders' patience wore thin. You should thank him. He actually told the detective about you being locked up in the storeroom."

"Ten minutes ago? You knew where we were ten minutes ago?"

Tom grinned. "You were safe and we wanted to make sure there were no more surprises."

Epilogue

HOMEWARD BOUND

"*A*re you riding in front with Edmonds?" Evie asked.

"Yes. I rather like the view from the front seat." Caro settled into the Duesenberg and looked up at Warwick Hall. "I had fun being Lady Carolina Thwaites but now I'm ready to return to my life."

"Pity." Evie smiled. "I had rather hoped Lady Carolina could accompany me to town when I next go in to outfit myself with a new wardrobe."

Caro tilted her head in thought. "I'm sure if you ask nicely, she would be happy to put in an appearance."

"How wonderfully accommodating."

Caro grinned. "This will be a story I can tell my grandchildren." Giving a small wave, she said, "Drive on, Edmonds."

Evie watched the Duesenberg make its way along the winding driveway. Turning to Sir Richard, she thanked him for his hospitality and offered him an invitation to visit Halton House.

"Send my regards to Lady Sara," he said.

"I most certainly will."

Isabel stepped forward and threw her arms around Evie. "Now, don't be a stranger." Jumping back, she added, "Oh, after our trip to Tuscany, we could stop by and visit you. Won't that be wonderful?"

Evie smiled until her jaw hurt. She knew she should have extended an invitation to Isabel but Evie wanted to believe she had left her friend in safe hands. Yes, indeed. Isabel would fare better with Sir Richard.

Evie waved to Phillipa who had already settled into her roadster.

When they were finally on their way, Evie sat back and tried to leave behind everything that had happened by switching her thoughts to Caro. She would lose her after all. Caro would meet someone and marry and have a family of her own. "I shall have to make sure she meets a perfect gentleman and doesn't move too far away."

"Pardon?" Tom asked.

"Oh, nothing. I'm just wishing for a perfect life." And trying to avoid thinking about Isabel visiting, she thought. "I can't help feeling sorry for Lark Wainscot. I hope she gets off lightly. At least, she won't be facing the gallows." The same couldn't be said for Lord Alexander Saunders.

"Have you given any thought to what you'll say to the dowagers?" Tom asked.

"I'm going to do my best to be evasive." She looked over her shoulder. "I'm glad Phillipa decided to return with us. I'm hoping she'll find other ways to gain life experience without putting herself at risk."

Tom laughed. "You think she'll be safe staying with you?"

Ignoring him, Evie said, "Why do return journeys always feel as though they take less time? I'm sure it took us twice as long to travel this distance before."

"I'm going to guess and say it's probably because you are eager to arrive and find out what the dowagers have been up to."

"Do you really think I have the power to influence time?" She shook her head. "Yes, I suppose you're right. I am eager to arrive. For all I know, I might be sleeping at the pub tonight because the dowagers have emptied out Halton House."

Tom gave her a worried look. "That means I'll be sleeping on a park bench because they only have one room available at the pub."

Evie laughed. "You're such a gentleman."

"So, you forgive me for keeping you locked up in the storeroom for longer than necessary. I really did want to make sure no one else would crawl out of the woodwork."

Evie lifted her chin. She hadn't broached the subject. In fact, she had deliberately avoided any mention of it. Instead, she had given Tom the cold shoulder. "I suppose you found it all too amusing. Will you tell my grandmother about it?"

"If I do, I will have to explain why you were cavorting with a criminal."

"Cavorting? Is that what you call having a conversation and asking pointed questions which, in time, would have led to his capture."

A while later, Tom said, "If you continue biting your thumb, you'll chew your way right through to the bone."

"I'm sure you can drive faster than this."

He pointed up ahead. "I can see the roof. That's

SONIA PARIN

something for you to be happy about. You still have a roof."

Evie craned her neck to look only to growl when the road dipped.

Finally, they drove through the Halton House gates and she saw Edgar standing at the porticoed entrance.

"Did you telephone ahead?" Evie asked.

"It didn't occur to me to do that. I'm sure Edgar had someone positioned as a lookout. Then again, Caro arrived before us."

As the motor car slowed, Edgar rushed toward it and trotted beside the passenger side saying, "My lady. We have been overwrought with concern. It is so good to see you alive and well."

Evie covered her face with her hands. Heavens. She knew Sir Richard had telephoned Sara and passed on the news about Lorenzo but it hadn't occurred to then contact the dowagers to set their minds at ease. Now she felt guilty.

"Thank you for your concern, Edgar. As you can see, we are quite alive and well." Turning to Tom, she said, "I'm going to change out of these clothes and then pay the dowagers a visit."

"I feel I have no choice but to join you."

"I'm ever so glad I didn't have to spell it out to you." Evie rushed inside only to stop and smile with appreciation. It felt wonderful to be home again, she thought.

She found Caro in her room busy unpacking her cases.

"Caro, please tell me you stopped to have a break."

"I did, milady, but everyone in the kitchen had so many questions. I decided to come up for some peace and quiet."

"I wish I could do the same but I'm afraid I need to pay the dowagers a visit without any further delay. What do you suggest I wear? A suit of armor?"

Evie and Tom sat in the roadster staring at the dowager house.

"I don't know if I should feel puzzled or amused." Henrietta's butler had directed them to another address to a manor house nearby. "They are definitely trying to engage my attention and interest. Do you think I've been ignoring them?" She tried to remember who lived in the Lodge, a local Georgian manor house with a pretty garden located between the village and Halton House. "Maybe there's a new arrival I don't know about."

"There's only one way to find out."

"At one time, the Lodge had been used to house guests who couldn't be accommodated at Halton House, especially during the shooting season. We had a tenant living there for a number of years but, since the end of the war, it's been sitting empty." She turned to Tom. "Do you have any theories?"

He shook his head. "I only hope they have tea and cake. We missed lunch."

"How can you think of food at a time like this? The dowagers might be about to make a significant announcement that will impact the rest of my life."

"Perhaps they have taken over the house and set up a shop. Didn't Napoleon say something about the English being a nation of shopkeepers?"

"Please don't say that within their hearing. I'm sure

they'll take offense and if they don't they will certainly take a bite out of you with a sharp retort." Frowning, she asked, "What sort of shop would they set up?"

Tom laughed. "A furniture store to sell all your unwanted furniture."

"Or maybe Sara has decided to take up residence there. I have been wondering how they were getting along living together at the dowager house. They appeared to be enjoying each other's company but I have been so preoccupied with my own life, I might have missed the signs of discontent." Evie pointed ahead and leaned forward. "There it is. The hedges have been trimmed and there are new drapes."

"You noticed the drapes?"

"They used to be a pretty shade of damask." She sat back and nibbled the edge of her lip. "Now they're brown. What can that possibly mean?"

Tom tipped his head back and laughed. "You are honestly reading too much into it. They're drapes."

"Oh, no. No. No. No. They are much more than that. Stay around long enough and you'll come to learn a thing or two about the way the dowagers think."

"Ready to face them?" Tom asked as he held the passenger door open.

"I guess there's no running away from this." Straightening, she lifted her chin. "Tally-ho."

Tom lifted the door knocker and gave it a light tap. The door opened and a butler Evie didn't recognize welcomed them and showed them through to the front parlor.

"Oh, our intrepid travelers have returned," Henrietta announced and gestured to the chairs opposite her.

"Sara. Henrietta." Evie sat on a chair that looked a

little familiar. As did the table next to it... and the book-cases and the vases.

"Tom Winchester. We hope you are pleased with the results." Henrietta handed him a cup of tea.

Evie accepted a cup from Sara and, before she took a sip, she looked at the cup. "This looks... familiar."

"Does it?" Henrietta shared a smile with Sara. "What do you think of the drapes."

"I told you they were new," Evie murmured. "They're... they're very masculine. Is that a hunting scene on the pattern?"

Henrietta looked quite pleased with herself. "What do you think of it?"

"It's... it's pretty, but I can't quite picture you living with it."

Henrietta looked puzzled. "Why would I do that?"

Sara looked amused. "You seem to be under the impression Henrietta will have to live with these drapes."

Evie looked from one to the other. "I'm sorry. I must be feeling travel weary." She turned to Tom who looked quite comfortable in an upholstered chair. Why would Henrietta care how Tom felt about the drapes?

"We have taken the liberty of moving all your luggage from the pub," Henrietta said. "Your butler has done a wonderful job of organizing it all."

"Tom? Is there something you wish to share with me?"

Tom grinned. "The dowagers offered to address your dilemma by setting me up in the Lodge. I believe I am now officially your tenant."

Henrietta leaned forward and murmured, "Although, he did offer to buy it outright. We know he is not accustomed to our ways and doesn't quite understand we do not sell land or property."

"I see. So... All that furniture you removed from Halton House..."

"Oh, we didn't think you would miss it. In fact, we were sure you would be pleased with the new arrangement."

Sara nodded. "I would have loved to stay on at Halton House but I have become quite accustomed to living at the dowager house with Henrietta."

Evie looked at Tom who shrugged.

He'd known. All along, he had known and he hadn't told her. He had listened to her prattling on about the dowagers suffering from kleptomania...

"More tea?" Henrietta offered.

"Oh, yes please."

Henrietta tipped the pot a fraction only to stop. "Oh, what with all the excitement of having you back I forgot about Sir Richard Warwick telephoning with such dreadful news about your friend's husband, Lorenzo Bianchi. We expected you to abandon the car rally straight away, but you stayed on..."

Evie knew she had just been given her cue to report on everything that had transpired over the last couple of days.

How much should she leave out?

"Well, there we were stranded at the Pecking Goose when Sir Richard came to our rescue..."

Evie decided she would skim through the story, sparing the dowagers anything that might give them a wrong impression of the bright young things or people in general. One couldn't go through life expecting the worst from people simply because they were different. Of course, in future, she would take more care…

"Yes, but how did you get a flat tire?" Henrietta asked. "You seem to have skipped that part." She looked at Sara who agreed.

"Yes, don't leave anything out."

Evie shrugged. "Oh, I thought you might be eager to hear about Lady Carolina Thwaites, but if you insist…"

"Oh, no… Do tell." Henrietta poured Evie a full cup of tea. "Who is Lady Carolina Thwaites?"

I hope you enjoyed reading Murder at the Car Rally. Next in the series: Book 4 - Murder in the Cards. If you wish to receive news about my new releases, please follow me on BookBub

Author Notes - Facts and Historical references

In my effort to ensure the story remained historically correct, I spent many hours checking and double-checking word and phrase usage. Here are some examples:

Decoration Day: The preferred name for the holiday gradually changed from "Decoration Day" to "Memorial Day", which was first used in 1882. Memorial Day did not become the more common name until after World War II, and was not declared the official name by Federal law until 1967.

Week-end: 1630s, from week + end. Originally a northern word (referring to the period from Saturday noon to Monday morning); it became general after 1878.

Getaway: 1852, "an escape," originally in fox hunting, from verbal phrase get away "escape". Of prisoners or criminals from 1893.

Pot-hole: 1826, originally a geological feature in glaciers and gravel beds. Applied to a hole in a road from 1909.

Like a bat out of hell: The Lions of the Lord: A Tale of the Old West By Harry Leon Wilson, Copyright 1903, published June, 1903, page 107 (google book full view):

Why, I tell you, young man, if I knew any places where the pinches was at, you'd see me comin' the other way like a bat out of hell.

Come clean: Moberly Evening Democrat, August 1904

Rain check: First recorded in 1880-1885

By hook or by crook: The phrase is very old, first recorded in 1380

Call it a day. (I wanted to use the phrase 'call it a night' but its first recorded use is 1938... The original phrase was "call it half a day", first recorded in 1838, which referred to leaving one's place of employment before the work day was over. The first recorded use of call it a day was in 1919, and of call it a night in 1938.

Play it by ear: The phrase 'play by ear' is much later. The first record of it is in an 1839 edition of The Edinburgh Review:

"Miss Austen is like one who plays by ear, while Miss Martineau understands the science."

Spitballing: US newspapers adopted the term in this sense from its use by baseball players, and have employed it frequently since at least 1903, at which time it prevailed against a competing term, 'wet ball', in use since before 1876:

...Simmons out at first; Abodie safe on muff of wet ball by Sullivan; J. Gleason and Galvin out on fly to Raja and Clinton.

Breakneck: extremely hazardous, likely to end in a broken neck 1560s

Haywire: first recorded 1920 Dialect Notes, Volume 82: Hay wire. Gone wrong or no good. Slang.

The Grass is Always Greener. A Latin proverb cited by Erasmus of Rotterdam was translated into English by Richard Taverner in 1545

Step up to the plate: The expression began to be used toward the end of the 19th century. One of the first recorded examples comes from the Illinois newspaper The Chicago Tribune, May 1874, in a game between the White Stockings and Hartford: The visitors were put out as fast as they stepped up to the plate.

Printed in Great Britain
by Amazon